NORA ROBERTS

OF
BLOOD
AND
BONE

pıatkus

PIATKUS

First published in Great Britain in 2018 by Piatkus
This paperback edition published in 2019 by Piatkus

1 3 5 7 9 10 8 6 4 2

A CIP catalogue record for this book
is available from the British Library.

ISBN: 978-0-349-41500-0

Printed and bound in Great Britain by
Clays Ltd, Elcograf S.p.A.

Papers used by Piatkus are from well-managed forests
and other responsible sources.

FSC
www.fsc.org

MIX
Paper from
responsible sources
FSC® C104740

Piatkus
An imprint of
Little, Brown Book Group
Carmelite House
50 Victoria Embankment
London EC4Y 0DZ

An Hachette UK Company
www.hachette.co.uk

www.littlebrown.co.uk

For Kayla,
who's growing up smart and strong

THE CHOICE

So nigh is grandeur to our dust,
So near is God to man,
When Duty whispers low, *Thou must*,
The youth replies, *I can*.

—RALPH WALDO EMERSON

Prologue

THEY SAID A VIRUS ENDED THE WORLD. BUT IT WAS magick, black as moonless midnight. The virus was its weapon, a barrage of arrows winging, silenced bullets striking, a jagged blade slicing. And yet the innocent—the touch of a hand, a mother's good-night kiss—spread the Doom, bringing sudden, painful, ugly death to billions.

Many who survived that first shocking strike died by their own hand or by another's as the thorny vines of madness, grief, and fear strangled the world. Still others, unable to find shelter, food, clean water, medications, simply withered and died waiting for help and hope that never came.

The spine of technology cracked, bringing the dark, the silence. Governments toppled from their perches of power.

The Doom gave no quarter to democracy, to dictators, to parliaments or kingdoms. It fed on presidents and peasants with equal greed.

Out of the dark, lights dimmed for millennia flickered and woke. The rise of magicks, white and black, sprang from the chaos. Awakened powers offered a choice between good and evil, light and dark.

Some would always choose the dark.

Uncannys shared what was left of the world with man. And those—man and magickals—who embraced the dark struck, turning great cities into rubble, hunting those who hid from them or fought against them to destroy, to enslave, to bask in blood even as bodies littered the ground.

Panicked governments ordered their militaries to sweep up survivors, to "contain" Uncannys. So a child who had discovered her wings might find herself restrained on a table in a lab, in the name of science.

Madmen claimed God in their vicious righteousness, stirring fear and hate to build their own armies to purge what was "other." Magick, they preached, came from the devil's hand, and any who possessed it were demons to be sent back to hell.

Raiders cruised the ruined cities, the highways, and the back roads to burn and kill because they enjoyed it. Man would always find ways to wreak cruelty on man.

In a world so broken, who would stop them?

There were murmurs in the light, rumblings in the dark, that reached the ears of men—of a warrior to come. She, daughter of the Tuatha de Danann, would remain hidden until she took up her sword and shield. Until she, The One, led light against the dark.

But months became years, and the world remained broken. Hunts and raids and sweeps continued.

Some hid, skittering out at night to scavenge or steal enough to survive another day. Some chose to take to the roads in an endless migration to nowhere. Others took to the woods to hunt, to the fields to plant. Some formed communities that ebbed and flowed as they struggled to live in a world where a handful of salt was more precious than gold.

And some, like those who found and formed New Hope, rebuilt.

When the world ended, Arlys Reid had reported it from the New York anchor desk she'd inherited. She'd watched the city burn around her, and in the end had chosen to tell the truth to all who could still hear her and escape.

She'd seen death up close, had killed to survive.

She'd seen the nightmares and the wonders.

She, along with a handful of people, including three infants, found the deserted rural town they had christened New Hope. And there they made their stand.

Now, in Year Four, New Hope was home to more than three hundred, had a mayor and town council, a police force, two schools—one for magickal training and education—a community garden and kitchen, two farms, one with a mill for flour and grain, a medical clinic—with a small dentistry— a library, an armory, and a militia.

They had doctors, healers, herbalists, weavers, sewing circles, plumbers, mechanics, carpenters, cooks. Some of them had made their living on those skills in the old world. Most studied and learned them in the new.

They had armed security posted around the clock. And though it remained on a volunteer basis, most all residents participated in combat and weapons training.

The New Hope Massacre, in their first year, remained a raw scar on their hearts and minds. That scar, and the graves of the dead, led to the forming of the militia and to the rescue parties who risked their lives to save others.

Arlys stood on the sidewalk, looking at New Hope, and saw why it mattered. Why all of it mattered. More than surviving, as it had been for those first horrible months, more even than building, as it had been for the months that followed.

It was living, and it was, like the town, hope.

It mattered, she thought now, that Laurel—elf—came out

to sweep the porch of the building where she lived on a cool spring morning. Up the street, Bill Anderson polished the glass on his shop window, and inside the shelves held dozens and dozens of useful things for easy bartering.

Fred, the young intern who'd faced the horrors of the underground out of New York with Arlys, would be busy in the community garden. Fred, with her magick wings and endless optimism, lived every day with hope.

Rachel—doctor and good, good friend—stepped out to open the doors of the clinic and wave.

"Where's the baby?" Arlys called out.

"Sleeping—unless Jonah's picked him up again when my back was turned. The man's bedazzled."

"As a daddy should be. Isn't today your six-week checkup, Doc? Big day for you."

"This doctor's already given her patient the all clear, but Ray's going to formalize it. Big day for you, too. How do you feel?"

"Great. Excited. A little nervous."

"I'll be tuning in—and I want to see you in here when you're done."

"I'll be there." As she spoke, Arlys laid a hand on the mountain of her belly. "This baby's got to be about cooked. Much longer, I won't even be able to waddle."

"We'll check it out. Good morning, Clarice," Rachel said as the first patient of the day came up the walk. "Come right on in. Good luck, Arlys. We'll be listening."

Arlys started to waddle—really, what other word was there—and stopped when she heard her name called.

She waited for Will Anderson—her childhood neighbor, current town deputy, and, as it turned out, the love of her life.

He laid a hand over hers on her belly, kissed her. "Walk you to work?"

"Sure."

He linked fingers with her as they walked to where he'd lived during his first months in the community. "Okay with you if I hang around and watch?"

"If you want, but I don't know how long it's going to take to set up. Chuck's optimistic, but—"

"If Chuck says we can do this, we can."

As her belly pinged with nerves, she let out a breath. "I've got to go with you there."

Chuck had been her primary source during the Doom, a hacker and IT genius who now ruled over what technology they had. In the basement, of course. The man was a confirmed basement dweller.

"I want to see you at work," Will added.

"What do you call what I do at home with the *New Hope Bulletin*?"

"Work, and a boon to the community. But we're talking live broadcast, baby. It's what you're meant to do."

"I know some people are worried about the risk, about drawing attention here. The wrong kind of attention."

"It's worth it. And Chuck not only knows what he's doing, but we'll have the magickal shields going. If you can reach one person out there, you can reach a hundred. If you can reach a hundred, who knows. A lot of people still don't know what the hell's going on, where to get help, supplies, medicine. This matters, Arlys."

It mattered, a great deal to her, when he risked his life on a rescue.

"I was just thinking about what matters." She paused outside the house, turned to him. "You're top of the list."

They circled around to the back of the house to the basement door.

Inside, what had been a large family room now stood as a computer geek's wet dream—if he dreamed of cobbling together components, cables, hard drives, motherboards, gutting ancient computers, reconfiguring desktops and laptops, hanging various screens.

She figured Chuck did.

He sat at one of the keyboards in a hoodie and cargo pants, a backward ball cap on hair recently bleached white courtesy of the community beautician. He'd gone bright red on his pointed little beard.

In the theme of bright red, Fred's curls bounced as she popped up from where she'd been sitting with three four-year-olds and an array of toys.

"Here's the talent! I'm production manager, gofer, and assistant camera."

"I thought I was the gofer." Katie, mother of three, kept an eye on them from the arm of the sagging sofa Arlys knew Chuck often slept on.

"Co-gofer, and supervisor of the power boosters."

Katie looked at her twins, Duncan and Antonia. "They're excited. I just hope they—and everybody—know what we're doing."

"We make it go for Arlys and Chuck," Duncan said, grinning at his mom. "Me and Tonia."

"Push!" Tonia giggled, lifting a hand. Duncan pressed his palm against hers. Light glowed.

"Not yet."

Hannah, blond and rosy against the twins' dark hair, got up. She patted her mother's leg, as if in comfort, then walked to Arlys. "When's the baby come out?"

"Soon. I hope."

"Can I watch?"

"Ah . . . "

On a laugh, Katie rose to swing Hannah up and kiss her. "She probably would."

"I don't know about that, kiddo." Chuck swiveled around in his chair. "But you're about to watch history, and the debut of New Hope Broadcasting."

"We're up?"

He grinned at Arlys, gave her a finger salute. "We're up. Definitely up with some help from our boosters."

The twins jumped up, eyes alight.

"Not yet, not yet." This time Arlys held them off. "I need to look over my notes, and . . . things. I need a few minutes."

"We're not going anywhere," Chuck told her.

"Okay, um, just give me a few."

Rattled when she hadn't expected to be, she walked back outside with her folder of notes. Fred walked out behind her.

"You shouldn't be nervous."

"Oh Jesus, Fred."

"I mean it. You're so good at it. You were always good at it."

"I got the desk in New York because everybody died."

"You got the desk when you did because of that," Fred corrected. "You'd have gotten it anyway, later, but anyway."

Stepping closer, Fred put her hands on Arlys's shoulders. "Do you remember what you did that last day?"

"I still have nightmares about it."

"What you did," Fred continued, "when Bob held a gun on you, on live TV. You held on. And what you did when he killed himself right there, right there sitting next to you? You held on, and more. You looked straight into the camera and you told the truth. You did it without notes, without the teleprompter. Because it's what you do. You tell people the truth. That's what you're going to do now."

"I don't know why I'm so nervous about this."

"Maybe hormones?"

Rubbing her belly, Arlys laughed. "Maybe. Hemorrhoids, heartburn, and hormones. Having a baby's an adventure."

"I can't wait to have my adventures." On a sigh, Fred looked over the back garden. "I want a zillion babies."

Arlys hoped she'd get through having this one—and soon. But right now, she had a job to do.

"Okay. Okay. How do I look?"

"Amazing. But today, I'm also your makeup artist. I'm going to powder you for the camera and do your lipstick, then you're going to be great."

"I love you, Fred. I really do."

"Aw. I love you back, I really do."

She let Fred powder and paint, did a few tongue twisters, sipped some water, did some yoga breathing.

When she came back in from the bathroom, she saw her father-in-law on the sofa surrounded by the children. He had a way of drawing them.

"Bill, who's minding the store?"

"Closed it for an hour. I want to see my girl live and in person. Your folks would be proud of you. Your mom, dad, Theo, they'd be proud."

"Consider this your anchor desk." Chuck tapped a chair in front of one of his many tables. "You're going to face this camera. I've got the angle. What we're doing here, boys and girls, is a fu—a freaking simulcast. We got the ham radio, the live-streaming, and the cable TV going. I'll be monitoring you and doing what I do over there. But pay no attention to the man behind the curtain. It's your show, Arlys."

"All right." She sat, adjusted. Opening her folder, she took out the photo of her last Christmas with her family. She propped it against a keyboard. "I'm ready when you are."

"Fred's going to give you the countdown. Okay, kids, let's make it boom."

"Don't say 'boom'!" Katie threw up her hands. "You have no idea."

"We make it go." Tonia wiggled her butt in delight. "We make it push, Duncan."

"Push." He grinned at his sister, they linked hands. Light shimmered through their fingers.

"That's what I'm talking about!" Chuck dashed from monitor to monitor, adjusted, let out a whoop. "That's what I'm saying. We're a go, and I mean *go*."

"Arlys." Fred moved behind the camera. "In five, four . . ."

She used her fingers to finish the countdown, and with a brilliant smile swept the last one forward.

"Good morning, this is Arlys Reid. I don't know how many can hear me, or see me, but if you're receiving this, pass the word. We'll continue to broadcast as often as possible, to give you information, to give you truth, to report. To let you know, wherever you are, you're not alone."

She took another breath, pressed her hands to her belly.

"Four years after the Doom, sources confirm Washington, D.C., remains unstable. Martial law remains in effect through the metropolitan area while gangs known as Raiders and the Dark Uncanny continue to attack. Resistance forces broke through security at a containment center in Arlington, Virginia. According to eyewitness accounts, more than thirty people were liberated."

She spoke for forty-two minutes. Reporting of the bombings in Houston, the Purity Warrior attack on a community in Greenbelt, Maryland, fires set, homes raided.

But she ended with stories of humanity, courage, and kindness. The mobile medical clinic that used wagons and horses to reach remote camps, shelters for the displaced, rescues, and food banks.

"Stay safe," she said, "but remember, it isn't enough to stay safe. Live, work, gather together. If you have a story, if you have news, if you're searching for a loved one and can get word to me, I'll report it. You're not alone. This is Arlys Reid for New Hope Broadcasting."

"And we're clear." Chuck stood up, pumped his fists. "Fucking A."

"Fucking A," Duncan echoed.

"Oops." Roaring with laughter as Katie just closed her eyes, Chuck jumped over to Duncan and Tonia, held out his fist. "Hey, totally awesome, kids. Fist bump. Come on! Fist bump."

Their heads tipped together as they both lifted their tiny fists, knocked them against his.

His sparked. "Whoa!" He danced around a little, blowing on his knuckles. "Major power surge. I *love* it."

Fred blinked at tears. "It was you-know-what A, and awesome."

Will bent over, kissed the top of Arlys's head. "You stagger me," he told her.

"It felt . . . right. Once I got over the hump, it just felt right. How long was I on?"

"Forty-two awesome minutes."

"Forty-two." She swiveled in her chair. "I shouldn't have kept the twins at it so long. I'm so sorry, Katie, I just lost track."

"They were fine. I kept track," Katie assured her. "They're

going to need a nice long nap." She glanced toward Hannah, curled up and sleeping in Bill's lap. "Like their sister. You look like you could use one. That had to take a lot out of you. You look a little pale."

"Actually, I think about five minutes in, I think I started having contractions. Maybe actually before that. I thought it was nerves."

"You—what? Now?"

Arlys gripped Will's hand. "I'm pretty sure we should go see Rachel. And I think it's— Okay!"

She braced one hand on the table, and squeezed Will's hand—bone against bone—with the other.

"Breathe," Katie ordered, hurrying over to lay a hand on Arlys's rock-hard belly, and began to rub in circles. "Breathe through it—you took the classes."

"Classes my ass. It doesn't hurt like this in classes."

"Breathe through it," Katie said again, calmly. "You just did the first New Hope simulcast while in labor. You can breathe through a contraction."

"It's easing off. It's easing."

"Thank you, Jesus," Will muttered and flexed his aching fingers. "Ow."

"Believe me, that's not even close to ow." Arlys blew out a strong breath. "I really want Rachel."

"Me, too." Will levered her up. "Let's take it slow though. Dad?"

"I'm having a grandchild."

Katie lifted Hannah from his lap. "Go with them."

"I'm having a grandchild," Bill repeated.

"Fred?" Arlys looked back. "Aren't you coming?"

"Really? I can? Oh, oh boy! I'll run over and tell Rachel. Oh boy! Chuck."

"Oh, no, thanks. I'll pass. No offense, Arlys, but, uh-uh."

"None taken."

"We're having a baby!" Fred spread her wings and flew out the basement door.

Duncan walked to the door to watch them all go. "He wants to come out."

Katie shifted Hannah. "He?"

"Uh-huh." Tonia walked over to stay with Duncan. "What's he doing in there?"

"That's another story," Katie told her. "Come on, kids, time to go home. Good work, Chuck."

"Best job ever."

OVER THE NEXT EIGHT hours Arlys learned a number of things. The first, and most urgent for several of those, was that contractions got a lot harder and lasted a hell of a lot longer as labor progressed.

She learned, not with any surprise, that Fred was a cheerful and tireless co-coach. And Will—no surprise, either—was a rock.

She got reports—a fine distraction—that her broadcast had reached at least the twenty miles out where Kim and Poe had traveled with a laptop on battery.

She sure as *fuck* learned why they called it labor.

At one point she dissolved into tears and had Will wrapping his arms around her. "It's almost over, baby. It's almost over."

"Not that, not that. Lana. I thought of Lana. Oh God, Will, oh God, to have to do this alone. Without Max, without Rachel, without us. To be alone and doing this."

"I don't believe she was alone." Fred stroked a hand down Arlys's arm. "I really, really don't. On the night—I could feel it. A lot of us could. The birth of The One. She wasn't alone, Arlys. I know it."

"Promise?"

"Cross my heart."

"Okay. Okay." When Will brushed her tears away, she managed a smile. "Almost over?"

"He's not wrong. Time to push," Rachel told her. "Will, support her back. Next contraction, push. Let's get this baby into the world."

She pushed, panted, pushed, panted, and eight hours after she made broadcast history, Arlys brought her son into the world that was.

She learned something more. Love could come like a bolt of light.

"Look at him! Look at him." Exhaustion fell away in stupefied love as the baby cried and wiggled in her arms. "Oh, Will, look at him."

"He's beautiful, you're beautiful. God, I love you."

Stepping back, Rachel rolled her aching shoulders. "Will, do you want to cut the cord?"

"I ..." He took the scissors from Rachel, then turned to his father, saw the tears on his cheeks.

He'd lost grandchildren in the Doom. A daughter, a wife, babies.

"I think Granddad should. How about it?"

Bill swiped fingers under his glasses. "I'm honored. I'm a grandfather."

As he cut the cord, Fred swept the room with rainbows. "I'm an aunt, right? An honorary aunt."

"Yes, you are." Arlys couldn't take her eyes off the baby. "You, Rachel, Katie. The New Hope originals."

"His color's excellent." Rachel took a good visual study.

"I'm going to need to take my nephew in a minute. Clean him up for you, weigh and measure him."

"In a minute. Hello, Theo." Arlys pressed a kiss to the baby's brow. "Theo William Anderson. We're going to make the world a better place for you. We're going to do all we can do to make it a better place. I swear it."

She traced Theo's face with her finger—so tiny, so sweet, so hers.

This is life, she thought. This is hope.

This is the reason for both.

She would work and fight every day to keep the promise she made to her son.

Holding him close, she thought again of Lana, of the child Lana had carried.

Of The One who was promised.

Chapter One

ON THE FARM WHERE SHE'D BEEN BORN, FALLON SWIFT learned how to plant and grow and harvest, to respect and use the land. She learned how to move through fields and forests, silent as a shadow, to hunt and fish. To respect the game, and take no more than needed, to take none at all for sport.

She learned to prepare food grown or taken from the land in her mother's kitchen or over a campfire.

She learned food was more than eggs fresh from the henhouse or a well-grilled trout. Food meant survival.

She learned to sew— though she disliked the time spent sitting still plying a needle. She learned how to tan leather, far from her favorite lesson, and could, if given no choice, spin yarn. Clothes, she learned, weren't simply something to wear. They protected the body, like a weapon.

She respected weapons, and had learned from a young age how to clean a gun, sharpen a knife, string a bow.

She learned how to build, with hammer and saw, to keep the fences in repair, to make repairs on the old farmhouse she loved as much as the woods.

A strong fence, a sound wall, a roof that held back the rain offered more than a happy home. They, too, meant survival.

And, though she often simply knew, she learned magicks. How to light the flame with a breath, how to cast a circle, how to heal a small wound with the light inside her, how to look, and how to see.

She learned, though she often simply knew, magick was more than a gift to be treasured, a craft to be honed, a weapon to be used with great care.

It was, and would be, survival.

Even with food, with shelter, with clothing and weapons, even with magicks, not all had survived. Not all would in the times to come.

She learned of a world that had existed before her birth. A world crowded with people, a world of huge cities with towering buildings where people had lived and worked. In that world people had traveled routinely by air and sea and road and track. Some had even traveled into space, and to the moon that hung in the sky.

Her mother had lived in a great city, in the City of New York. Fallon knew from the stories told, from the books she devoured, it had been a place full of people and noise and light and dark.

A wonder of a place to her, one she vowed to see someday.

She imagined it often at night when she lay awake watching the faeries dance outside her window.

There had been war in that world, and bigotry and cruelty, just as there was now. She knew of the wars that had been from the books, from the stories. And she knew of the wars that were still raging from visitors who stopped at the farm.

Her father had been a soldier once. He had taught her to fight—with her hands, her feet, her mind. She learned how to read maps and how to make them, and imagined following them one day on the journeys she knew, had always known, she would take.

She had no attachment, as her parents did, to the world that had been before the Doom had killed so many. Billions, it was said. Many remembered when those great cities fell to the burning, the mad things, the dark magicks. The cruelty and greed of men still swam in the minds and the blood of those who'd lived through it.

When she caught glimpses of tomorrows, she knew there would be more burning, more blood, more death. And she would be part of it. So she often lay awake at night, cuddling her teddy bear, a gift from a man she'd yet to meet.

If those tomorrows weighed too heavy, she sometimes slipped out of the house while her parents and siblings slept, to sit outside while the little faeries flickered like fireflies. Where she could smell the earth, the crops, the animals.

Most often she slept the quiet and innocent sleep of a child with loving parents and three annoying little brothers, a healthy child with a questing mind and an active body.

Sometimes she dreamed of her sire, the man her mother had lived with in New York, the man she'd loved. The man, Fallon knew, who had died so she would live.

He'd been a writer, a leader, a great hero. She bore his name, just as she bore the name of the man who brought her into the world, who raised her, who taught her. Fallon for Max Fallon, her sire. Swift for Simon Swift, her father.

Two names, Fallon thought, equally important. Just as her mother wore two rings, one from each man she'd loved.

And though she loved her father as deeply and truly as any child could love, she wondered about the man who'd given her the color of her eyes and hair who, along with her mother, had passed powers to her with their mating.

She read his books—all books were gifts—and studied the photo of him on the back of them.

Once, when she was only six, she'd curled up in the library with one of Max Fallon's books. Though she couldn't understand all the words, she liked that it was about a wizard, one who used magicks and brains to fight against evil forces.

When her father came in, a stab of guilt had her trying to hide the book. Her dad had no magicks, but he had a lot of brains.

He'd plucked her and the book up, then sat to hold her on his lap. She loved how he smelled of the farm—the earth, the animals, the growing things.

Sometimes she wished she had eyes like his that changed from sort of green to sort of gold or just mixed those colors together. When she wished it, she felt guilty about Max.

"It's a good book."

"You read it?"

"Yeah. My mom really liked to read. It's why she and my dad made this room for books. You don't have to hide anything from me, baby. Not anything."

"Because you're my daddy." She turned into him, pressed her face to his heart. *Beat, beat, beat.* "You're my daddy."

"I'm your daddy. But I wouldn't have gotten the chance to be if it wasn't for Max Fallon." He turned the book over so they could both look at the picture of the dark, handsome man with strong gray eyes. "I wouldn't have my most beautiful girl if he hadn't loved your mom, and she hadn't loved him. If they hadn't made you. If he hadn't loved her and you enough, been brave enough, to give his life to protect you. I'm real grateful to him, Fallon. I owe him everything."

"Mama loves you, Daddy."

"Yeah, she does. I'm a lucky guy. She loves me, and she loves you, and Colin and Travis."

"And the new baby that's coming."

"Yeah."

"It's not a girl." This on a huge, sorrowful sigh.

"Is that so?"

"She has a boy in her, again. Why can't she make a sister for me? Why does she always make brothers?"

She heard the laugh in his chest as he cuddled her. "Actually, that's supposed to be my job. I guess it's the way it goes."

He stroked her long black hair as he spoke. "And I guess that means you'll just have to go on being my favorite girl. Have you told your mom it's a boy?"

"She doesn't want to know which kind. She likes the wondering."

"Then I won't tell her, either." Simon kissed the top of her head. "Our secret."

"Daddy?"

"Hmm?"

"I can't read all the words. Some are too hard."

"Well, why don't I read the first chapter to you before we go back to chores?"

He shifted her so she could curl up, then opened the book, turned to page one, and began.

She hadn't known *The Wizard King* had been Max Fallon's first novel—or perhaps some part of her had. But she would remember, forever, that her father had read it to her, chapter by chapter, every night before bed.

SO SHE LEARNED. SHE learned about goodness from her father, generosity from her mother. She learned about love and light and respect from the home and family and life given to her.

She learned of war and hardship and grief from travelers, many wounded, who came to the farm or to the village nearby.

She had lessons on politics, and found them annoying, as people talked too much, did too little. And what good were politics when reports claimed the government—such a vague word to her—had begun to rebuild in the third year after the Doom, only to fall again before the end of Year Five?

Now, in the twelfth year, the capital of the United States—which didn't seem united to Fallon, then or now—remained a war zone. Factions of the Raiders, groups of the Dark Uncanny, and those faithful to the cult of the Purity Warriors battled for power, for land, for the smell of blood. Against each other, it seemed, and against those who sought to rule or govern.

Even though Fallon wanted peace, wanted to build, to grow, she understood the need, the duty to fight to protect and defend. More than once she'd seen her father arm himself and leave the farm to help protect a neighbor, to help defend the village. More than once she'd seen his eyes when he'd come home again, and had known there'd been blood, there'd been death.

She'd been raised to fight, to defend, as had her brothers. Even as the farm basked in summer, as the crops ripened and fruit hung heavy, as the woods ran thick with game, bitter battles raged beyond the fields and hills of home.

And her time, her childhood, she knew, was counting down like the ticks of a clock.

She was The One.

On days when her brothers deviled her—why had she been plagued with brothers?—when her mother understood *nothing* and her father expected too darn much, she wanted that countdown to hurry.

Other times she raged. Why should she have no choice? No choice? She wanted to hunt and fish, to ride her horse, to run in the woods with her dogs. Even with her brothers.

And often she grieved for what something beyond her, something beyond her parents, demanded she become. Grieved at the thought of leaving her family, her home.

She grew tall and strong, and the light within her burned bright. The thought of her thirteenth birthday filled her with dread.

She stewed about it—about all that was unfair in her world, all that was unfair in the world outside—as she helped her mother prepare the evening meal.

"We're going to get a storm tonight, I can feel it." Lana pushed at the butterscotch-blond hair she'd bundled on top of her head before cooking. "But it's a perfect evening for eating outside. Go ahead and drain those potatoes I've got parboiling."

Fallon sulked over to the stove. "Why do you always have to do the cooking?"

Lana gently shook a covered bowl. Inside slices of peppers fresh from the garden marinated. "Your dad's grilling tonight," she reminded Fallon.

"You made everything first." With that stuck in her craw, Fallon dumped chunks of potatoes into the colander in the sink. "Why doesn't Dad or Colin or Travis make it all?"

"They help, just like you. Ethan, too—he's learning. But to answer the point of your question: I like to cook. I enjoy making food, especially for my family."

"What if I don't?" Fallon whirled around, a tall, long-limbed girl currently all stormy-gray eyes and defiant scowl. "What if I just don't want to cook? Why do I have to do things I don't want to do?"

"Because we all do. Lucky for you, on next week's rotation you move from under chef to cleanup. I need you to season those potatoes for the grill basket. I already chopped the herbs."

"Fine, great." She knew the drill. Olive oil, herbs, salt, pepper.

Just as she knew they had the oil and spices because her mother and a witch from a neighboring farm had culled out three acres, and had cast a spell to turn it into the tropics. They'd planted olive trees, *Piper nigrum* for pepper, coffee beans, banana trees. Figs, dates.

Her dad had worked with others to construct olive presses for the oils, dryers for the fruits.

Everyone worked together, everyone benefited. She *knew* that.

And still.

"Why don't you go ahead and take those out, tell your dad to start the chicken?"

Leading with her foul mood, Fallon stomped out of the house. Lana watched her daughter, her own summer-blue eyes clouding. She thought: More than one storm's coming.

They ate at the big outdoor table her father had built, using colorful plates, with bright blue napkins and wildflowers in little pots.

Her mother believed in setting a pretty table. She let Ethan light the candles with his breath because it always made him laugh. Fallon plopped down beside Ethan. She didn't consider him as much a pain in her butt as Colin or Travis.

Then again, he was only six. He'd get there.

Simon, his mop of brown hair streaked from the sun, took his seat, smiled at Lana. "It looks great, babe."

Lana lifted her wine, made from their own grapes. "Credit

to the grill master. We're grateful," she added, with a glance at her daughter, "for the food grown and made by our own hands. We hope for the day when no one goes hungry."

"I'm hungry now!" Colin announced.

"Then be grateful there's food on the table." Lana set a drumstick—his favorite—on his plate.

"I helped Dad with the grill," he claimed as he added potatoes, vegetables, an ear of just-shucked corn to his plate. "So I shouldn't have to do the dishes."

"That's not going to fly, son." Simon filled Travis's plate as Lana did Ethan's.

Colin waved his drumstick in the air before biting in. He had his father's eyes, that hazel that blurred gold and green, hair a few shades darker than his mother's going bright from the summer sun. As usual, it stood up in tufts that refused taming.

"I picked the corn."

Travis, already eating steadily, elbowed Colin. "We picked it."

"Irrelement."

"Vant," Simon corrected. "Irrelevant—and it's not."

"I picked most of the corn. It should count."

"Instead of worrying about the dishes—which you will do—maybe you should eat the corn," Lana suggested as she helped Ethan butter his ear.

"In a free society, everybody has a vote."

"Too bad you don't live in one." Simon gave Colin a poke in the ribs that had Colin flashing a toothy grin.

"The corn is good!" Ethan, though he'd lost a couple of baby teeth, bit his way enthusiastically down the ear. He had his mother's blue eyes, her pretty blond hair, and the sunniest of dispositions.

"Maybe I'll run for president." Colin, never one to be

deterred, pushed forward. "I'll be president of the Swift Family Farm and Cooperative. Then the village. I'll name it Colinville and never wash dishes again."

"Nobody'd vote for you." Travis, nearly close enough in looks to be Colin's twin, snickered.

"I'll vote for you, Colin!"

"What if I ran for president, too?" Travis asked Ethan.

"I'd vote for both of you. And Fallon."

"Leave me out of it," Fallon rebuked, poking at the food on her plate.

"You can only vote for one person," Travis pointed out.

"Why?"

"Because."

" 'Because' is dumb."

"This whole conversation is dumb." Fallon flicked a hand in the air. "You can't be president because, even if there were any real structure of government, you're not old enough or smart enough."

"I'm as smart as you," Colin tossed back, "and I'll get older. I can be president if I want. I can be anything I want."

"In your dreams," Travis added with a smirk.

It earned him a kick under the table, which he returned.

"A president is a leader, and a leader leads."

When Fallon surged to her feet, Simon started to speak, to shut things down, but caught Lana's eye.

"You don't know anything about being a leader."

"You don't know anything about anything," Colin shot back.

"I know a leader doesn't go around naming places after himself. I know a leader has to be responsible for people, make sure they have food and shelter, has to decide who goes to war, who lives and dies. I know a leader has to fight, maybe even kill."

As she raged, shimmers of light sparked around her in angry red.

"A leader's who everybody looks to for answers, even when there aren't any. Who everyone blames when things go wrong. A leader's the one who has to do the dirty work, even if it's the damn dishes."

She stalked away, trailing that angry light into the house. Slamming the door behind her.

"Why does she get to act like a brat?" Colin demanded. "Why does she get to be mean?"

Ethan, tears swirling in his eyes, turned to his mother. "Is Fallon mad at us?"

"No, baby, she's just mad. We're going to give her a little time alone, okay?" She looked over at Simon. "She just needs some space. She'll apologize, Colin."

He only shrugged. "I can be president if I want. She's not the boss of the world."

Lana's heart tore a little. "Did I mention I made peach pie for dessert?" Pie, she knew, was a no-fail way to turn her boys' moods around. "That is, for anyone who clears his plate."

"I know a good way to work off that pie." In tune with Lana, Simon went back to his meal. "A little basketball."

Since he'd created a half court on the side of the barn, basketball had become one of his boys' favorite pastimes.

"I wanna be on your team, Daddy!"

Simon grinned at Ethan, gave him a wink. "We'll wipe the court with them, champ."

"No way." Colin dived back into the meal. "Travis and I will crush."

Travis looked at his mother, held her gaze a long moment.

He knows, Lana thought. And so did Colin, even if anger and insult blocked it away.

Their sister wasn't the boss of the world, but she carried the weight of it on her shoulders.

FALLON'S TEMPER BURNED OUT in a spate of self-pity tears. She flung herself on her bed to shed them—the bed her father had built to replicate one she'd seen in an old magazine. Eventually the tears died away into headachy sulks.

It wasn't fair, nothing was fair. And Colin started it. He always started something with his big, stupid ideas. Probably because he didn't have any magicks. Probably because he was jealous.

He could have her magicks, then he could go off with some stranger to learn how to be the savior of the whole stupid world.

She just wanted to be normal. Like the girls in the village, at the other farms. Like anyone.

She heard the shouts, the laughter through her open window, tried to ignore it. But she rose, looked out.

The sky held blue on that long, late summer day, but like her mother, she felt a storm coming.

She saw her father, with Ethan perched on his shoulders, walking toward the barn. The older boys already raced around the curve of blacktop in the basketball shoes their father had scavenged.

She didn't want to smile when her dad nipped the ball from Colin, held it up for Ethan, then walked Ethan to the basket so he could drop the ball through the hoop.

She didn't want to smile.

The older boys looked like Dad, Ethan looked like Mom. And she looked like the man on the back of a book.

That alone often cut more than she thought she could stand.

She heard the soft knock on her door, then her mother

came in. "I thought you might be hungry. You barely touched your dinner."

Shame began to push through the sulks. Fallon only shook her head.

"Later then." Lana set the plate on the dresser Simon had built. "You know how to warm it up when you're ready."

Fallon shook her head again, but this time tears spilled. Lana simply walked to her, drew her in.

"I'm sorry."

"I know."

"I spoiled everything."

"You didn't."

"I wanted to."

Lana kissed Fallon's cheek. "I know, but you didn't. You'll apologize to your brothers, but right now, you can hear they're happy. Nothing's spoiled."

"I don't look like them, or you, or Dad."

Lana ran a hand down Fallon's long black ponytail, then eased back to look into those familiar gray eyes.

"I've told you about the night you were born. It's always been one of your favorite stories." As she spoke, she guided Fallon to the bed, sat on the side of it with her. "I've never told you about the night you were conceived."

"I . . . " Heat rose to her cheeks. She knew what *conceived* meant, and how it happened. "That's — It's weird."

"You're almost thirteen, and even if we hadn't already talked about all of this, you live on a farm. You know where babies come from and how they get there."

"But it's weird when it's your mom."

"A little weird," Lana allowed, "so I'll ease you into it. We lived in Chelsea. That's a neighborhood in New York. I loved it. There was a sweet little bakery across the street, a good deli on the corner. Pretty shops close by, lovely old buildings. We had a loft—I moved into Max's loft. I loved that, too. There were big windows facing the street. You could see the world rush by. Shelves full of books. The kitchen wasn't nearly as big as the one here at home, but it was completely up-to-date. We often had dinner parties with friends.

"I worked at a good restaurant, and had some vague plans about opening my own one day."

"You're the best cook."

"Not a lot of competition for that now." Lana tucked an arm around Fallon's waist. "I came home from work, and we had some wine, some really good wine, and made love. And after, only minutes after, something just burst inside me. Such light, such glory, such . . . I can't explain the feeling, even now. It took my breath, in the most beautiful way. Max felt it, too. We joked about it a little. He got a candle. My gift had been so small that even lighting a candle was hit-and-miss, and only hit after a lot of effort."

"Really? But you—"

"Changed, Fallon. Opened, that night. I lit the candle with barely a thought. It rose in me, the new power. As it did in Max, in all of us who had magicks inside. But for me, what I had inside was you. That moment, that burst, that glory, that light was you. I wouldn't know for weeks, but it was you. You sparked inside me that night. I came to know, and some you showed me while still inside me, that you aren't just special to me, to Max, to Simon, but to all."

"I don't want to go away." Fallon buried her face in Lana's shoulder. "I don't want to be The One."

"Then say no. It's your choice, Fallon. You can't be forced, and I'd never allow anyone to force you. Your father would never allow it."

She knew this, too. They'd told her, always, it would be her decision. But ... "You wouldn't be disappointed in me? Ashamed of me?"

"No." Lana pulled Fallon close, held her tight. "No, no, never." How many nights had she raged and grieved over what would be asked of this child? This *child*. Her child. "You're my heart," Lana comforted. "I'm proud of you every day. I'm proud of you, your mind, your heart, your light. Oh God, it burns so bright. And I'd take that light from you without hesitation to spare you from making the choice. From having to make it."

"He died to save me. My birth father."

"Not just because of what you might be. Because he loved you. Fallon, you and I? We're the luckiest women. We've been loved by two amazing men, two courageous men. Whatever you decide, they and I will love you."

Fallon held on, comforted, eased. Then felt ... She drew carefully back. "There's more. I can feel it. I can feel there's more, things you haven't told me."

"I told you about New Hope, and—"

"Who's Eric?"

Lana jerked back. "Don't do that. You know the rule about pushing into another mind."

"I didn't. I swear. I just saw it. Felt it. There's more," Fallon said, and now her voice trembled. "More you're not telling me because you're worried. You're afraid for me, I can feel it. But if you don't tell me everything, how will I know what to do?"

Lana rose, walked to the window. She looked out at her boys, at her man, at the two old dogs, Harper and Lee, sleeping in the sun. At the two young dogs running around the boys. At the farm, the home she treasured. At the life she'd built. Dark always pushed against the light, she thought with some bitterness.

Magick always demanded a price.

She'd kept things from her child, from the brightest of lights because she feared. Because she wanted her family together, at home. Safe.

"I kept things from you because, under it all, I wanted you to say no. I told you about the attack when we lived in the house in the mountains."

"Two who were with you turned. They were Dark Uncanny, but you didn't know until they tried to kill you. To kill me. You and Max and the others fought, and thought you'd destroyed them."

"Yes, but we hadn't."

"They attacked again in New Hope. They came for me, and to save you, to save me, Max sacrificed himself. You ran like he told you to do. You ran because they'd come back again, and you had to protect me. You were alone a long time, and they hunted you. And you found the farm, you found Dad."

Fallon took a breath. "Was this Eric one of them? One of the dark?"

"Yes. He and the woman he was with, the woman I think helped turn him away from the light. They wanted to kill me, to kill you. They killed Max. Eric is Max's brother."

"His brother?" Shock ran straight through her. Brothers, she thought, horrified, however irritating, were *brothers*. They were family. "My uncle. My blood."

"Eric chose to betray that blood, chose to kill his own brother. Chose the dark."

"He chose," Fallon murmured. After another breath, she squared her shoulders. "You need to tell me all of it. You can't leave anything out. Will you tell me?"

"Yes." Lana pressed her fingers to her eyes. She already knew, looking into those familiar gray eyes, what choice her child would make. "Yes, I'll tell you everything."

Chapter Two

FALLON APOLOGIZED. COLIN SHRUGGED IT OFF, BUT since she knew from experience he held a grudge, she prepared for retaliation. With her birthday—and the choice—only weeks away, she preferred thinking about her brother's revenge.

That was normal, that was family.

And she preferred the calculation in his eyes to the worry she often saw in her mother's, her father's.

She helped cut hay and wheat, harvest fruit and vegetables. Daily chores helped keep her steady. She didn't complain about the kitchen work—or only muttered about it in her head. The end of summer and the coming of fall meant hours of making jams and jellies, canning that fruit and those vegetables for the winter to come.

A winter she dreaded.

When she could, she escaped, using her free time to ride the fields and the woods on her beloved horse, Grace. Named for the pirate queen Fallon had long admired.

She might ride to the stream just to sit and think—her baited hook in the water was an afterthought. If she brought home fish to eat or to barter, so much the better. But the hour or two of solitude fed her young, anxious soul.

She might practice little magicks there—calling the butterflies, making the fish jump, spinning little funnels of air with her fingers.

On a hot day of bold sun and stingy breezes that seemed to claim summer would never end, she sat in her favorite spot. Because she wanted to read, her fishing pole hung magickally suspended over the stream.

She could make the fish bite the bait, but such powers—she'd been taught—were only to be used to feed real hunger.

Birds called now and again. She heard an occasional rustle in the understory. If she hadn't been deep in her book, she would have tested herself to identify the sounds. Deer, rabbit, squirrel, fox, bear. And more rarely, man.

But she enjoyed letting herself slide into a story—a really scary one—about a young boy with a gift, with a shining (a light), trapped in an old hotel with evil.

She didn't pay attention to the plop of the water, even when it repeated. Not when the bushes shaped like animals outside the evil hotel moved, not when they threatened the boy.

But the gurgling voice got her attention.

Her heart, already racing from the story, gave one hard *thud* as she heard her name whispered in that watery voice. And the water in the stream rippled.

Cautiously, she set the book aside and rose, one hand on the knife in her belt.

"What magick is this?" she murmured.

Was it a sign? Was it something dark come to call?

Her name came again, and the water seemed to shudder, to writhe. Butterflies that had danced along the water's edge swarmed away in a buttercup-colored cloud.

And the air went silent as a grave.

Well, she wasn't a little boy in a book, she reminded herself, stepping closer to the edge of the stream.

"I'm Fallon Swift," she called out over the beat of blood in her ears. "Who are you? What do you want?"

"I have no name. I am all names."

"What do you want?"

A single finger of water rose up from the rippling stream. It only took her a second to recognize which finger, and the meaning. But it was a second too late.

They hit her from behind, three against one. She face-planted in the water, then surfaced to the sounds of her brothers' hilarity.

After she swiped her dripping hair out of her eyes, she found the bottom with her feet, stood.

"It took three of you, and an ambush."

" 'Who are you?' " Colin repeated in a quaking voice. " 'What do you want?' You should've seen your face!"

"Nice to see how you accept apologies."

"You deserved it. Now we're even."

Maybe she had deserved it, and she had to give him credit for biding his time, enlisting his brothers. Even more, she had to admire the complexity and creativity of the trick.

But.

She considered her options, the humiliation if she failed, and decided to take the risk.

She'd been practicing.

While her brothers laughed and did their victory dance, she spoke to her horse, mind to mind. Moving forward, Grace head-butted Colin into the water.

"Hey!" Shorter than Fallon, he tread water, managed to find his footing. "No fair."

"Neither is three against one."

Mad with laughter, Ethan jumped in. "I wanna swim, too."

"What the heck." Travis toed off his shoes, cannonballed in.

While the boys splashed and dunked each other, Fallon rolled over to float. This time she spoke mind to mind with Travis.

This was your work.

Yeah.

I apologized.

Yeah, but he needed this. And it was fun.

He turned his head, smiled at her.

Plus, it's a hot day.

The middle finger was rude.

But funny.

She couldn't hold back her own smirk. *But funny. I need a few minutes alone with Colin.*

Jeez, it's just water.

Not about that. Even steven. I just need a few minutes.

His gaze sharpened on hers. He saw, he knew, as he usually did. He started to speak out loud, then turned away. Only nodded.

She waded out of the stream, climbed out. After whisking her hands down her body to dry off, she stowed her book, her rod.

"We have to get back," she called out.

She ignored the whining—mostly Ethan's—gave a come-ahead gesture. "We've got to help with dinner, start the evening chores."

Travis climbed out; Fallon dried him off.

"Thanks."

She had to crouch down to help Ethan out.

"It's funny to swim in your clothes."

She poked him lightly in the nose. "It wouldn't be so funny if you had to walk home in wet, squeaky shoes."

She dried them, then his pants, then the faded Under Armour shirt she knew had once been scavenged for Colin.

After taking up Grace's reins, she turned to Colin.

"Come on." He waved a hand at her. "You paid me back for paying you back."

"I'll dry you off if you give me your word you're not going to pay me back for paying you back."

He hesitated for a minute, then just grinned. "I had a good one I'm working on, but I can save it until the next time you're a bitchy bitch. Probably won't take long."

She stuck out her hand. "But this round's done."

"Done."

They shook on it.

Dry again, he glanced around. "Why'd they take off?"

"I told Travis I needed to talk to you."

Suspicion and retaliation gleamed in his eyes. "We said done and shook."

"Not about that." She began to walk, the horse plodding lazily behind. "It's almost my birthday."

"Yeah, yeah."

"My thirteenth birthday."

"So?" With a shrug he found a stick to bang on trees as they walked. "You're probably going to start kissing boys and putting bows in your hair. Dopey."

"I'll have to leave."

"And you're going to get to drive the truck. I could drive the truck. I don't see why you get to do everything first."

"Colin, I won't be here to drive the truck. I'll have to go."

"Go where?"

She saw the knowledge flash over his face. Her parents hadn't held the story of Mallick, of The One, of two years of training away from home a secret.

Furious denial immediately followed knowledge. "That's bullshit. You're not going anywhere. That's just a bull-shit story."

He liked to swear, Fallon thought idly. He swore at every opportunity out of their parents' hearing.

"It's not. And when he comes, I'll have to go with him."

"I said bullshit." Furious, red-faced with it, Colin heaved the stick away. "I don't care who this weird guy is, he's not going to make you go. We'll stop him. I'll stop him."

"He won't make me. He can't make me. But I have to go with him."

"You *want* to go." Bitter now. So young, so bitter now. "You want to go off and pretend you're some big-deal Savior. Pretend you're The One who's going to save the world. Just more bullshit."

He shoved her, hard.

"You're not so damn special, and there's nothing wrong with the stupid world. Look at it!"

He flung out his hands to the thick woods, the dappled sunlight, the verdant peace of late summer.

"This isn't the world, just our part of it, and even that may be threatened."

It rose up in her, rose so fast, so hot, it left her breathless. "You look at it. See the world."

She lifted her hands, flung them apart like whipping open a curtain.

A battle raged, dark and bloody. Buildings in rubble, others aflame. Bodies, torn and mangled, lay across ... sidewalks, she realized. Streets and sidewalks of a city, a once great city.

Gunfire ripped across the still woods, and screams followed. Lightning struck, black and red, exploding chasms where more fell.

Some flew on wings that slashed through flesh. Some flew on wings that tried to shield.

Uncannys, dark and light, people, good and evil, waging war over the blood of those already fallen.

"Stop it." Colin gripped her arm as she stood, transfixed. "Stop it, stop it."

He sobbed the last, got through.

Shaking, she whipped the curtain closed again.

"How did you do that? How did you do that?"

"I don't know." Queasy now, dizzy with it, Fallon slid down to sit on the path. "I don't know. I feel sick."

He yanked her canteen out of her saddlebag and, crouching, pushed it at her.

"Drink some water. Drink it and maybe put your head between your knees."

She sipped, shut her eyes. "I see it in my head sometimes. When I sleep mostly. Like that, or other places. It's always fighting and dying and burning. Sometimes I see people in cages, or on tables, strapped down on tables. And worse, even worse."

She capped the canteen. "I'm okay now. I don't know how I did that. I don't know enough."

He helped her to her feet, put the canteen away for her. "Where was that place?"

"I'm not sure. I think it was Washington, D.C., but I don't even know why I think that. I don't know enough. It's why I have to go. I have to learn more, I have to, and I'm afraid. I'm so scared. They want to kill me, they tried to kill me and Mom. They killed my birth father. They'll find me sooner or later. They could come here and find me. If anything happened to Mom and Dad, to you and Travis and Ethan . . ."

She turned to her horse, pressed her face to Grace's neck.

"I have to go and learn how to stop them or it won't ever stop."

Awkwardly, Colin patted her back. "I'll go with you."

"You can't."

"Just try to stop me." The bullheaded bravery, the sincerity and innocence of it, sprang back. "You think because I can't do stupid tricks and all that crap I can't fight? I'm going with you, you jerk."

It touched her, she didn't know if she could ever tell him how much, that at her lowest point, he stood up for her. "It's not because of magick." And, even at so young an age, she understood basic tactics. "It's not because you wouldn't fight."

She wiped at tears, turned, saw he'd shed tears of his own.

"You have to stay because you have to be president."

"What the fuck?" Even with his newfound love of swearing, Colin reserved the Big F for his most important cursing.

"It's like this." Steadier, she began to walk again. "Mom and Dad are like the king and queen, right? They rule. But they don't know everything that goes on. They'll know about the stream today unless you guys swore Ethan to secrecy. If he's not sworn, he'll blab."

"Damn it."

"So they'll know, but that's okay. Nobody's mad about it. But they don't know everything, and the oldest—that's going to be you—has to be in charge, too. You have to be president and look out for Travis and Ethan, and Mom and Dad, too. I need to know everybody's going to be okay. Please. It's a hard job. You have to make sure everybody's okay, everybody does their chores and lessons. And you can't be too bossy about it or it doesn't work."

He hip-bumped her as they walked. "You're bossy."

"I could be bossier. Lots. Please, Colin."

They stopped at the rise where so long before their mother had first looked down at the farm, first felt hope again.

"I can be president," he mumbled. "I already told you I could."

"Okay."

She draped an arm over his shoulders, and for a few moments they looked down at home.

Ethan fed the dogs, the old and the young. Travis walked along a row in the garden, filling a basket with green beans. Their father, head shielded by a cap, walked back from a near field with one of the horses, and their mother straightened from her work in the herb bed to wave at him.

She'd take this picture with her, Fallon thought. This and others, wherever she had to go. Whatever she had to do.

DAY AFTER DAY, NIGHT after night, Lana watched her children with a kind of wonder. Before the Doom, she'd never given more than a passing thought to having children—someday. She'd enjoyed the life she'd lived, the urban glint of it, with a man she'd loved and admired.

She'd dabbled in magicks mostly for the fun, and her powers had been barely whispers in any case. Or so she'd believed.

Her work satisfied her, so ambitions for more had been, like children, a passing thought for someday.

She'd lived with a writer whose books had found a solid niche. Max had taken the Craft more seriously than she had, and his powers had been more overt—but still, in those days a pale shadow of what would come.

Their love had still held the bright shine of the new and exciting, and the future—if she looked beyond a day or two—had seemed limitless.

Then the world ended. Everything she'd taken for granted,

gone in smoke and blood and the screams of circling crows. With the life that sparked inside her that night in January, another world began.

In those months between that winter night and the bold summer day she'd first seen the farm, she'd changed into someone the contented urban woman wouldn't have recognized. Changed, she knew, not just with the child growing inside her, not just with the rise of her own powers, but fundamentally.

Just as the hungry, desperate, grieving woman Simon found raiding his henhouse for an egg had changed into the woman who lay sleepless in her husband's arms on a cool autumn night listening to the incessant hooting of an owl.

This woman had learned to love not only for days and weeks and months, but for years. She had planted fields, hunted game, embraced her power. She'd given birth to four children in the bed she shared with the man who'd helped her bring them into the world.

Their world.

But she knew the world beyond this farm, this haven. She'd lived in it, fought in it, survived it. Escaped from it.

And now, after all the loss, the gains, the grief and the joy, she faced sending her firstborn into that blood and smoke.

Simon stroked her back. "We can say no."

She nuzzled a little closer. "Reading my mind now?"

"It's not hard when we're on the same page. She's just a kid, Lana. Yeah, it was important for us to be straight and honest with her from the jump, not to wait and just spring all this on her, but she's still just a kid. We sit her down, make sure she knows we've got her back on this. She doesn't have to go."

"We never lied to her, or kept secrets. And still, I think she'd have known even if we had. It's in her, Simon. I felt it when I carried her. I feel it now."

"Remember that time, her first spring? We were working in the garden. We had her napping in the shade under the old apple tree with Harper and Lee. We looked over when we heard her laughing and there must've been a couple hundred butterflies and—"

"Faeries, those little lights." At the pretty memory, Lana could smile. "All dancing around her. She called them."

"She couldn't even walk yet. I know she's not a baby anymore, but, Jesus, she's only twelve years old."

Thirteen, Lana thought. In only days now.

Absently she twisted the chain that held the medal of Michael the Archangel, which he wore around his neck. "She's decided to go."

"You don't know that."

She only spread her hand over his heart.

Under her palm, Simon's heart tore a little. He lifted his hand to take hers.

They'd promised each other to stand united when the day came, and, whatever choice she made, to stand with Fallon.

"I guess that explains why she hasn't been fighting with the boys. Has she talked to you about it?"

"No, not with words. I know she was born for what's about to begin. I know it with all I am. And I hate it." She turned her face into his throat. "She's our baby, Simon. I hate it."

"We can find a way to stop it, stop her."

Lana shook her head, burrowed deeper. "It's beyond us, Simon. It always has been. Even if we could, what happens when the boys grow up, when they need a life beyond this farm? Do we keep them here forever, like treasures caught in amber? We've been able to give them the life we have, to keep them safe, because of Fallon. Because we were given this time."

"Time's up, I get it. I know how to defend what's mine, Lana."

"You proved that to me before I was yours. But we can't fight this. I'm yours." She lifted her head to look at him, laid a hand on his cheek. "As Fallon's yours, as the boys are. I'm not strong enough, we're not strong enough, to face this without you. We have to let her go." A tear spilled out. "Help me let her go."

He shifted, sat up, gathered her close so she could weep a little. "Here's what I know for sure. She's smart and she's strong and, hell, she's fucking wily on top of it."

Lana managed a watery laugh. "She is. She really is."

"Between us, we've taught her everything we know, and she already had a pretty big leg up there, too. It's two years." He squeezed his eyes shut as his heart tore a little more. "Time's going to go fast, and she's going to be fine. It's like wizard boarding school, only she already knows more than Harry Potter."

She sighed now, comforted. "Simon."

"What do you say we make the rounds?"

"Yeah." Lana dashed away tears, shook back her hair. "That's a good idea."

She thought of the house, that square, sturdy house she'd seen from the rise. How he'd opened it to her and the child she'd carried.

They'd added to it over the years—the man could build. They'd opened a wall in the living room to add space for necessities like sewing, spinning, weaving. They'd added sheep to their stock. They'd added space to the kitchen for canning, preserving. And a second greenhouse for growing through the winter.

And while they'd built, she thought as she wrapped herself

in a robe, they'd filled the bedrooms with babies. That tangible proof of love and hope, those precious lights.

Together they'd built a family, and kept it safe—within that amber, she admitted. Together, they'd given their girl the best foundation they knew how to give.

Now together they walked first to the room Travis and Ethan shared. Moonlight streamed through the windows onto the bunk beds Simon had built.

Travis sprawled belly down on the top bunk, one arm flung over the edge and the soft cotton blanket she'd bartered for with two jars of pickles, made from her own cucumbers, knotted around his feet.

Though it would end up there again, she moved into the room to spread the blanket over him.

On the lower bunk Ethan slept in a cheerful puppy pile with the two young dogs, Scout and Jem. He smiled in his sleep.

"He'd have half the animals on the farm in bed with him if he could get away with it," Simon whispered.

"Piglets," she said, making him laugh.

"I still don't know how he got those three piglets past both of us."

"He has such a kind heart. And this one." Gently, she lifted Travis's arm back onto the bed. "He loves his pranks, but he sees so much, knows so much."

"He's a damn good farmer."

She smiled, stepped back. "Like his daddy."

After one last look, they backed out and walked over to Colin's room.

Curled on his side, he had one hand clutched on his blanket as if someone might try to steal it from him while he slept.

His odd assortment of found items filled a wooden box on his dresser or stood on his windowsill and on the shelves Simon had hung for him.

Interesting pebbles or stones, some green glass smoothed and polished by time in the stream, a clump of dried moss, a quarter, a few pennies, a broken pocketknife, an old bottle cap, the dented top of a thermos, and so on.

"Nobody scavenges better," Simon commented.

"It's his gift, seeing the potential for treasure. I know sometimes he resents not having the abilities like the others, but he has that curious mind."

"And plenty of ego. Colinville."

Smiling, she bent to kiss Colin's cheek. "President Swift of Colinville doesn't smell like a little boy anymore. Travis and Ethan still have that wild, innocent scent. Now, with him, there's a hint of gym locker. Healthy and male."

She turned, slid into Simon's arms. "I wonder if Colinville will ever have gym lockers."

"Since his first act as chief executive will be the construction of a basketball court, gym lockers follow."

She tipped her face up to his. "You're so good for me."

He kissed her, lingered. "You know what we should do?"

"Didn't we already do that?"

"Bears repeating. But I was thinking, we should get John Pike to come over with that old film camera he's got, and take a family portrait. He's got that darkroom set up, and the last I heard he still has the supplies."

"And you have to barter your left leg for a photo."

"I can talk him down from that. Trust me."

"I always have, and I'd love to have a photo."

They left Colin sleeping, walked down to Fallon's room. Faeries flickered outside her window as they often did.

She slept facing them with one hand resting on the pink teddy bear.

Mallick's other gifts, the candle, the crystal, stood on the dresser with *The Wizard King*. Moving closer, Lana saw Fallon held a little wooden horse in her other hand.

"You made that for her first Christmas." She turned into him again. "You want the photo for her, so she can take it with her."

"John can make two. She's so damn pretty, isn't she? Sometimes I look at her, and it just stops my heart. And I think, all I really want is to be able to scare off the boys that'll come around, at least until I figure one's good enough for her. Like when she's thirty or forty. Maybe fifty. I'd like to be able to bitch at her how she's wearing too much makeup or her skirt's too short or—"

Lana squeezed hard. "You've given her everything a father could and should." She eased back, cupping his face because she saw pain in his eyes. "The night she was born. Into your hands. Into yours, Simon. She'll always reach for your hands."

Breathing out, she took his hand now. "She'll come back to us. I couldn't let her go if I didn't know that. She'll come back to us."

But for how long, and what happened between, what happened after, she couldn't see.

Chapter Three

ON FALLON'S THIRTEENTH BIRTHDAY, THE WOODS SPLASHED vibrant against the sky. Fruit not yet harvested hung heavy on the branches of the apple and pear trees. Grapes grew in fat, glossy clusters on the vine.

The garden spread autumn color with pumpkins, squash, zucchini, plump cabbages, rows of kale and turnips.

The air held warm, but cool nights warned the first frost would come, and soon.

Simon put the boys on apple-picking duty, as it gave them an excuse to climb the trees. As she had the best hand for it, he had Fallon harvesting grapes for jellies, wine, eating, and drying. He knew Lana had already baked the spice cake—Fallon's favorite—and now worked the garden, gathering more of the harvest while he stacked firewood for the winter to come.

And everyone pretended it was just an ordinary day because they could do nothing else.

He listened to his boys laughing, the low hum of the chickens, the deeper hum from the beehive. He felt the sweat dampen his back, the fatigue of muscles as he hauled another log to the splitter.

Somewhere in the woods, a woodpecker drummed manically. The dogs ignored the beat as well as the deer that roamed along the ridge as they slept in a flood of sun.

Situation normal, he thought, all fucked up.

Once, he'd chosen a soldier's life, and he'd learned the cost of war. He'd given up that life and come home to the farm when his mother was diagnosed with cancer. He'd learned a great deal about love, sacrifice, and a woman's strength.

She'd beaten the cancer, only to fall to the virus. So he'd buried both his parents within days of each other, and had learned the pain of real loss.

He'd chosen to stay, to farm, and learned what he and others could do to make a life even while the world shifted out from under them. And what others could and would do to bring more death, more destruction.

More than once over the years, he'd helped a neighbor fight off those others. And he'd buried friends as well as enemies.

He'd seen crows circling in the distance, beyond their quiet acres. He'd seen the lightning flash black.

Now his daughter would go beyond him, into that dark and dangerous world. And he, a man, a solider, a father, was helpless to stop it.

He looked over at her, his long, lanky, lovely girl. The sun glinted on the dark braid down her back. She wore one of his mother's old gardening hats, a wide-brimmed straw. The faded blue shirt had been his mother's, too, and showed that his girl had sprouted what Lana called booblets.

He didn't like to think about it.

He'd bartered for the jeans—on the baggy side, as she was so slim—and the sturdy brown boots.

He wanted to hold her there, just like that. Standing in the little vineyard, a bunch of ripe purple grapes in her hand, her face lifted up to the sun.

With his eyes still on her, he hauled up the split wood to add to the stack. He saw her stiffen, watched her turn slowly, her face blank—a mask of control no one so young should wear.

She set the grapes in her basket, slid the clippers into the sheath on her belt, and began to walk down the terraced rows of the vineyard.

Everything went silent. The laughter of the boys, the hum of bees and chickens. The dogs didn't bark. Simon felt for a moment, one long, breaking moment, the world stopped breathing.

His did.

Mallick stood at the edge of the farm road, holding the reins of his horse. The same horse he'd ridden thirteen years before, Simon would swear it. He looked the same as well, not a day older, the dark hair waving down, the white streak in his beard.

Lana stood in the garden, one hand pressed to her heart, the other fisted at her side.

Simon dropped the wood on the ground, rushed forward.

"Dad." Her voice steady, her eyes dry, Fallon stopped to reach for his arm.

Until she had, he didn't realize he had a hand on the gun in his belt.

"You should get Ethan," she told him. "He's crying."

"Baby."

"I'm okay. I need you to help me do this. Please, please, Daddy, help me do this."

The mask slipped; his daughter's eyes pleaded with him. "Go to your mom first. I'll get the boys."

So she went to her mother, took Lana's hand. Together they walked to Mallick.

"Lady," he said, "the years sit well on you, and on this land."

"A choice, you said. You can't make her go."

"Mom."

Already grieving, Lana rounded on Fallon. "I'm your mother. I decide. You're not old enough to make a choice like this. You don't know what's out there. You don't—"

She broke off when Fallon's arms came around her, when Fallon spoke in her head.

I know what you know. I've seen what you've seen. I've dreamed what you've dreamed. Help me do this. Help me be strong like you. Let me go so I can be what you helped make me. Let me go so I can come back.

Fallon drew back, but kept her mother's hand as she faced Mallick.

"Have you chosen, Fallon Swift?"

"Will they be safe while I'm gone? I won't leave my family unless I know they'll be safe."

"No harm comes to them while you train with me."

"If it does, you'll pay for it."

He nodded. "Understood. Simon Swift." Absently he patted one of the dogs who sniffed at him as Simon led the boys up. Mallick scanned the boys, the grim-faced Colin, the cool-eyed Travis, Ethan, who knuckled away tears. "You've made fine sons. May I water my horse while you say good-bye?"

"Now? But she hasn't had her cake or her gifts. I—I have to help her pack."

"Mom. I'm packed. I'm ready. I'll go get my things."

Saying nothing, Simon gestured Mallick to the water trough by the barn.

"I . . . I need to pack some food. She needs to have her cake."

Lana escaped into the house.

"Go get your presents for your sister," Simon told the boys. He crossed to Mallick. "Where are you taking her?"

"Not as far as you fear, not as near as you might wish. I can't tell you more, for her safety."

"And how do we know she's safe?"

"You know duty, and she's my duty. Believe me, I would lay my life down for her. Not for love, as you would, but for duty that's as strong in me. She is my purpose, my hope, my duty. I will not fail her."

"You know duty," Simon repeated. "Believe me, if harm comes to her, I will hunt you down whoever and whatever you are. And wherever you are, I will find you and I will kill you."

"If harm comes to her, Simon Swift, I will already be dead. And what is left of the world will wish for the same fate. In two years she'll come back to you, and you'll see what you helped her become."

"Two years from now, if she's not back safe, I'll come for you."

He strode away, stopping short when Fallon came out with a small duffel bag. "I need to saddle Grace."

"I'll do it." Travis rushed out. "I'll do it. I made you this."

He offered her a leather sheath for her knife, one with symbols carefully burned into the leather.

"They're magick symbols to keep the blade sharp and clean, and to help it strike true."

"It's really beautiful, Travis. You ... must've worked on it a long time."

"I know you have to go." When his voice thickened, he swallowed. "I know you're afraid, but you'll come back."

"Yes. I'll come back."

"You'll be different, but you'll come back. I'll bring Grace."

She started to speak to her father, struggled for what she wanted to say. Colin and Ethan came out and spared her.

"I don't want you to go." Ethan flung his arms around her legs. "Don't go away."

"I have to, for a while, and I need you to do something for me." She opened her bag, took out the pink bear. "I need you to take care of her, okay? She really needs to be snuggled at night."

"You should take her with you."

"She doesn't want to go. She wants to stay here. Will you take care of her until I get home?"

"I won't let anything happen to her. I made you this. Well, mostly Dad made it, but I helped, and I said make a flower, and I painted it. It's a birthday flower."

She took the little wooden tulip painted bright and inexpertly pink and green. "It's really pretty. Thanks, Ethan."

She crouched to tuck it into her bag, then unbuckled her knife sheath to replace it with her new one.

"I did this." Colin shoved a little box at her.

From inside, she lifted out a small wind chime. Thin white stones, pieces of smooth colored glass hung from fishing wire attached to an old metal hook.

"It's beautiful."

"It's stupid, but—"

"It's beautiful."

She saw tears in him, barely held back, and hugged him hard. "You're the president now," she whispered. "Don't forget."

When her mother came out, Fallon saw the signs of weeping even through the glamour.

"There's some of your cake, and bread from this morning, some meat and cheese, and . . . Well, here's Travis with Grace. I'll put this in your saddlebag."

"I'll do it." Colin took the food pack, and the duffel.

"It's so fast," Lana murmured. "It's all too fast."

Afraid she'd lose her nerve, Fallon bent down, hugged Ethan. "Take care of the bear, and don't let the big guys push you around."

She straightened, turned to Travis, held tight. "Don't even think about moving into my room."

Then to Colin. "Try not to be such a big jerk."

"You're the jerk."

"Try not to screw up too much while I'm gone."

She stepped back, turned to her mother. "Mom."

"This is from your dad and me."

Fallon reached for the chain that held what she knew was her father's wedding ring and her dad's St. Michael's medal. Tears and love flooded her throat.

"I'll always wear it." She slipped the chain around her neck. "Always. Mom." She fell into her mother's embrace. "I love you. I love you so much."

"I love you. I'll think of you every day, and count the days off until you're home again. Shine bright, my baby, and I'll know. Send me a sign," Lana whispered.

"I will."

Fighting tears, she turned into her father's arms. "Daddy. I love you."

"If you need me. Listen." He cupped her face, lifted it. "If you need me, call for me. I'll hear you. I'll come to you. I'll find a way."

"I'm not afraid because I have you. I'm not afraid because you love me. I'll come home." She pressed her cheek to his. "I swear it."

She grabbed the reins, launched into the saddle. "My fifteenth birthday, don't forget. I want presents."

She set Grace into a trot. Mallick, already mounted, rode up to her, gestured south.

She turned, one more look, saw her family standing together, close, touching, in front of the house where she'd been born.

Colin straightened his shoulders, sent her a snappy salute that made her lips curve, her eyes blur.

She lifted her hand into a wave, then turned her eyes south and urged Grace into a gallop.

MALLICK LET HER SET the pace. He could give her free rein for a few miles, see how long it took for her to steady herself. And his sturdy old bay could handle the run.

They passed another farm, smaller than the Swifts', where a woman and a skinny boy dug for potatoes. They paused in their work, and in the few seconds it took to thunder by, Mallick felt a wave of longing from the boy.

For the girl, and for what the boy saw as freedom.

They galloped on, past a scatter of abandoned houses with lawns gone back to meadows. A few sheep grazed on the rock-pocked hills, and their elderly shepherdess stood on a mound with an old-fashioned crook in one hand and a rifle slung over her back.

The image of her, gray hair under a worn cap, the rough gray rocks pushing out of the green, the white sheep mindlessly cropping, brought him a quick, unexpected tug of nostalgia.

When Fallon slowed to a trot, then a walk—more for her horse's sake than her own, Mallick concluded—she turned for the first time to look at him directly.

"I want to know where we're going."

"A day's ride and a bit more, to a place where you'll train and learn and grow."

"Why are you the one to train me?"

"That is a question I can't answer. Why are you The One? We are what we are."

"Who gave you the authority?"

"This you'll learn. Who is the shepherdess?"

"Her name's Molly Crane."

"And what is her power?"

If she wondered how he knew old Molly had power, she didn't ask. "Shapeshifter."

"How many sheep was she tending?"

Fallon answered first with an annoyed shrug. "Maybe ten."

"'Maybe'?"

"I didn't count them."

"You have eyes. How many did you see?"

"I don't know."

"You didn't look, so didn't see. Fourteen. One stood behind a rock, and the pregnant ewe carries two."

Grief and nerves fought a bitter war in her belly. Her sharp, slapping tone to an adult would have earned her a rebuke at home.

But she wasn't home now.

"What difference does it make?"

"Another time you may see the enemy. How will you know their number? One may hide behind a rock, another may conceal two others."

Angry, aching, she sneered at him. "The next time I have to fight sheep, I'll be sure to get the full count."

Mallick gestured east. Far over the rolling hills, crows circled. "They know the waiting time is done. You'll be hunted, from this day until the end."

"I'm not afraid of crows."

"Be afraid of what rules them. Fear can be a weapon just

as courage. Without fear there is no prudence. Without prudence there is recklessness. With recklessness, defeat."

"What rules them?"

"You'll learn."

With that, he urged his horse up a rise and into the trees.

The air cooled, and though she'd never traveled this far from home, the scents of the forest had a comforting familiarity. She passed some time watching for tracks, identifying the deer, a lone bear, a coyote, and a pair of raccoons that had passed over the rough trail.

They crossed a narrow stream where water bubbled and spilled over rocks. A wild turkey called as they veered east.

"How many deer were in the shadows by the stream?" she demanded, adding a cool stare when he turned his head to study her. "What if they were enemies? Would you know their number?"

"Four does and two yearlings."

"What's the difference in the yearlings?"

Amused, Mallick answered, "One is a young buck, the other a doe."

"Besides that."

Now his eyebrows lifted. "I cannot tell you."

"One has a sore left front leg. He's favoring it. Didn't you see the tracks? Isn't it good tactics to know if your enemy's injured?"

"You have a good eye for tracking. If your aim is as keen, we'll eat well this winter."

"My aim's true. My father taught me." She lifted her hand to the chain around her neck, found comfort there. "I can still go home. I can change my mind and go home."

"Yes. You could live out your life there and never truly

become. And the world would bleed around you until even what you love drowns."

She hated, hated, *hated* knowing—somehow knowing—he spoke absolute truth.

"Why do I have to be The One? Everybody's Savior? I didn't screw everything up, so why am I supposed to fix it?"

"Mae gennych atebion y tu mewn i chi."

"What? What language is that?"

"I said the answers are inside you."

"That's just the same as saying I'll learn. It's not an answer." However much she wanted to dismiss him, curiosity poked at her. "What language is it?"

"Welsh."

"Is that where you're from? Wales?" With the question she tried to form a map in her head, place it exactly. She loved maps.

"Yes. Do you know where that is in the world?"

"It's in what was Great Britain, with England on one side and the Irish Sea on the other."

"Very good. Your geography skills are accurate even if your language skills are poor."

"Why would my parents teach me Welsh? They don't *know* Welsh. And anyway, it's not like I'm going to just drop down over there."

Fueled by anger, aching, and now insulted for her family, her words shot out like barbs. "And they taught me plenty, me and my brothers. How to read and write and *think*. We learned science and math and history, how to read maps, how to draw them. Maybe we couldn't go to the school in the village very often because Raiders and Dark Uncannys could come too close. My dad fought them to help protect our neighbors, and he and Mom taught us how to fight, too."

"They taught you much, and they taught you of the light and of the earth. And a most important lesson. They taught you loyalty. You learned it well."

"You don't learn it. You are or you aren't."

He smiled at her. "However we might disagree, know I am loyal to you."

"Because you have to be, and that's different."

"You're right," Mallick said after a long moment. "But my loyalty remains."

She rode a few miles, stewing, until the questions just pushed out of her.

"Why did you leave Wales?"

"I was called."

Her sigh, long and derisive, said everything about being thirteen and dealing with an adult.

"If I ask who called you, you're just going to say 'you'll learn.'"

"And you will. I was young, like you, and like you I wondered why such hard things were asked of me. Know I understand what it is to leave home and family."

"Do you have kids?"

"I've never been given that gift."

"You brought me the teddy bear."

"It was kind of you to give it to your young brother, to leave that piece of yourself in his care."

She shoved that aside, as it brought Ethan and his tears to her mind.

"You brought me the candle and the crystal ball. They're not toys like the bear. Only I can light the candle. Sometimes I do. It never melts away."

"It was made for you."

"Did you make it?"

"Yes."

"My mother said I'd be the only one to see into the crystal, but I've never seen anything when I look."

"You will."

"Where did you get it?"

"I made it for you. The bear I bought for you before even your mother knew you existed. The woman at the shop told me it was a happy gift for a baby girl."

It occurred to her, as they rode, that she'd never had a longer conversation with anyone outside of family. While it didn't make her feel any warmer toward him, she did find it interesting.

"What are you going to teach me?" she demanded. "For two years? My father taught me how to shoot—a gun and a bow. He taught me hand-to-hand. He was a soldier. He was a captain in the army. And my mother taught me about magicks. She's a witch, a powerful witch."

"Then you have a good foundation for more."

She stopped her horse. "Do you hear that?"

"Yes."

"It's engines. More than one."

"There's a road, not far, and some travel on it. So we make our route through the trees, over the hills. You're not yet ready for battle."

The sounds receded, until only the forest spoke.

"Who taught you?"

"His name was Bran. A difficult taskmaster."

"Will I meet him?"

"He's no longer with us."

"Did he die in the Doom?"

His duty was to teach, to train, he thought, and he would fulfill it. But who could know the girl had so many questions in her?

"No, he passed from this world to the next long before. But while I was with him he taught me many things. I traveled to many lands with him."

Because she could, Fallon took Grace for a little jump over a fallen tree. "Before the Doom people traveled all over the world, in planes. I've seen two planes and a chopper—the smaller plane with blades on the top. My mother put a shield over the farm in case people in planes were the ones looking for Uncannys to lock them away. Or worse, Dark Uncannys. So we could see the planes, but they couldn't see us. Have you ever flown in a plane?"

"I have, and I didn't enjoy it."

"I think it would be wonderful." She tipped her head up, looked at the pieces of sky through the canopy of burnished leaves. "I'd like to see other lands. Some have beaches of white sand and blue water, and others are covered in ice. And the great cities with buildings tall as mountains, and mountains taller than the tallest building, and deserts and oceans and jungles."

"The world has many wonders."

He turned his horse through an opening in the trees and into a small clearing. A cabin sat sheltered under trees with a slope-roofed lean-to attached.

"You said a day's ride."

"And so it will be. We stop here only for the night."

"We've still got more than an hour before dusk."

"The horses need rest, to be tended and fed. And so do I."

Mallick dismounted, led his horse to the lean-to. Reluctantly, Fallon followed suit. She noted the shelter had fresh bedding, grooming supplies, a tub of grain. Mallick handed her a bucket.

"There's a creek just to the east. The horses need to be watered."

"What is this place?"

"A place to break our journey." When she said nothing, simply stood, he loosened the cinches, hefted off his saddle.

"A hunting cabin, what would have been a weekend or holiday sort of place. It belonged to a man who worked as a plumber and enjoyed coming here with his friends. He was immune, so survived the Doom only to be taken in one of the sweeps and confined to a government facility, where he died."

"You knew him?"

"No, but there was enough of his energy left here, where he had many happy times, for me to know of him. The horses need water."

She took the bucket, walked no more than ten yards east to a bright and cheerfully winding creek. For a moment, she studied the woods—this new place. The hemlock and oak, the old pines and young poplars. For all she knew, Mallick would ask her how many trees in the stupid forest. Or how many rapid taps from the woodpecker, how many feathers on the cardinal.

She filled the bucket, walked back to dump water in the trough. It took another two trips, and by then Mallick had removed both saddles and was toweling off his gelding.

"What's his name?" she asked as she got a clean towel to rub down her own horse.

"He's Gwydion, named for a powerful wizard and warrior."

"She's Grace, for the pirate queen. The lean-to is much newer than the cabin."

"I built it only a few months ago."

"It looks sound," she said, picking out Grace's hooves.

With the horses fed and watered, Mallick took up his own light pack. Fallon shouldered her heavier duffel and the food her mother had packed.

The cabin, a square and squat structure, included a narrow front porch up one short step.

Beside the step, in a pool of pebbles, stood a rough stone figure. Female, Fallon judged.

Mallick paused to open his water flask, and trickled some water over the pebbles.

"In tribute and respect for the goddess."

"Does she protect or bless?"

"She may do both, at her whim. She is Ernmas." He sighed a little when Fallon only frowned. "She is a mother goddess, she is of the Tuatha de Danann, as you are. You are of her blood and bone, Fallon Swift. Do you know nothing of your ancestors?"

"We had some books on mythology, mostly like the Romans and Greeks. You don't seriously expect me to believe I'm related to some goddess? Because, you know, *mythology*."

"Your ignorance does you no credit." He walked onto the porch, flicked a hand at the door. It opened with a rush of wind. "Do you think power—the light, the dark—has no source? Has no history or purpose? You owe what you are to all who came before you. To their bounty and their battles, their cruelty and their compassion." He shook his head. "That the fate of the world rests with a girl who knows so little."

As he walked inside, Fallon rolled her eyes behind his back. She looked down at the goddess. "How am I supposed to know what I don't know?"

Insulted—she was *not* ignorant—she stomped in behind Mallick.

Inside, the main area consisted of one open room with a fireplace on the north wall and a kitchen in the back— windows east, she noted, to overlook the creek, and catch the sunrise.

A big—and ugly to her eye—couch in some sort of black-and-brown plaid faced the TV over the fireplace. They had a TV at the farm, and once a week they had movie night with the DVDs.

She loved DVDs almost as much as maps, as both took you to other places, other worlds.

Two chairs, that same plaid, a table with a lamp with a black bear climbing a black tree for a base, an overhead light fashioned from some sort of cart or wagon wheel and a round wooden table with four wooden chairs filled the space in what she considered a really ugly way.

She took the food pack to the counter covered in a muddled gray over white, set it down.

"Your room for the night is on the left. Start the fire, then put away your things."

He wasn't the only one who could show off, she thought. She turned away, tossed a glance at the logs in the stone fireplace. They burst into flame.

"I'm not stupid."

"Ignorant," he corrected. "I've heard the expression 'you can't fix stupid.' It may be true. But ignorance can be educated. Put your bag in your room, then you'll need to bring in more firewood before dark. There's plenty out the back of the house."

"And what are you going to do?"

"I'm going to have a glass of wine before we share what your mother kindly provided."

When she stalked away, he looked at the fire, the bright, hot light of it, and smiled.

Chapter Four

PURE STUBBORNNESS MATED TO INSULT TEMPTED HER
to lock herself in the dumb room with its two sets of bunk
beds—covered in plaid again, this time red and black. But
she was hungry, and she had to pee.

So she'd pee, and she'd eat, but she didn't have to be
friendly. She didn't see why she had to be polite, either. He'd
called her stupid—oh, excuse me, *ignorant*. Just because he
was old didn't mean she had to be polite to somebody who
called her ignorant.

A bathroom stood directly across from her room. She did
lock herself in there.

She tested for running water by turning the handle on the
faucet over the wall-hung sink, and was almost disappointed
when it ran. She supposed Mallick had seen to that, so she
had no reason to test her powers there.

The toilet rocked a little, but served its purpose.

She took a moment to study her face in the mirror over
the sink. She hadn't slept well the night before—or the night
before that, she admitted. It showed in the shadows under her
eyes, a paleness to her cheeks.

Though she didn't care about looking pretty, she did

care—a lot—about looking strong. So she did a light glamour.

Not ignorant, she told herself, and not weak.

She strode out, sailed straight by Mallick as he sat near the fire with his glass of wine. She didn't slam the door on her way out for wood, but shut it with a solid *snap*.

As dusk fell, a soft gray sliding through the trees, the air carried a sharper chill. And the smell of the smoke, of the galloping fall.

The firewood would be welcome, she thought, but she wanted a walk first, wanted to stretch muscles tight after the hours in the saddle.

She checked on the horses first, found them already dozing. Still, she rested her cheek against Grace's for the comfort of home. And when Mallick's horse looked at her with kind, wise eyes, Fallon stroked him—and thought he deserved a nicer rider.

She let them go back to dozing and walked along the edge of the winding creek.

Glancing up, she saw the deer stand built on the thick oak, and found it amusing to watch five deer graze their way down the sloping land through the trees.

What would it be like, she wondered, to just keep walking? Like the deer. Just walk and live in the woods. To wander as long and far as she liked, with no thought but to her own needs.

No one to tell her what to do, she imagined, or when and how to do it. No one to expect so much of her when she just wanted to be.

She leaned on the tree, pressed her cheek to its rough bark. Felt its heartbeat. Closing her eyes, she felt the heartbeat of the deer across the little creek and the pulse of the water, the earth.

All the things that lived and thrived around her, and were not man, she felt their life inside her. In her mind's eye she saw the bird winging overhead, its heartbeat small and quick, small and quick. And the owl deeper in the woods, slumbering until night fell and hunting began.

She squeezed her eyes tighter because she understood she didn't just want to walk away, to live forever in the woods. She wanted to feel her mother's heartbeat, her father's, her brothers'. And they were too far away.

"It's just the first day," she admonished herself. "I can get through one day. I can change my mind, anytime I want. I can go home tomorrow if I want."

Comforted by that, she opened her eyes again, and turned to walk back to the cabin.

The sun burned through the trees to the west, flamed over the hills with a light that she felt, like the heartbeats, inside her.

Watching that fire of the day's end, she walked back, and brought in a load of firewood.

A TEENAGER, EVEN ONE descended from gods, knew how to sulk. Fallon ate the food Mallick set out, but she ate in silence. She took a small slice of her birthday cake because she wanted to feel her family close. But it only made her sad, only made her accept that they weren't close, and wouldn't be for two long years.

If Mallick had made any attempt to cheer her, that sadness would have lashed out as bright fury. Maybe he knew, as he offered no conversation or small talk through the simple meal.

When he told her to see to the dishes, she didn't argue. She repacked the food, washed the plates, ordered the kitchen, while he sat by the fire reading.

Despite her innate curiosity, she didn't ask about the book, but actually locked herself in the bedroom and added a charm to the lock, simply out of pique.

Though it invariably brought her comfort, she refused to take the candle out of her pack and light it simply because it had come from him. In her mind, in that moment, Mallick and Mallick alone held responsibility for her misery.

Instead, she huddled under the blankets with *The Wizard King*, illuminating pages as she read. But the familiar words only added more sadness.

She set the book aside, lay in the dark wishing she'd taken the time to hunt through the cabin for something else to read. Old magazines and newspapers never failed to fascinate her. She didn't expect to sleep, fully anticipated brooding through the night. Even looked forward to it.

And dropped off before she felt sleep sliding over her, not waking even when the moonlight shifted through the windows or the faeries came to dance outside the glass.

She woke at the trembling edge of dawn. Her first reaction was embarrassment that she'd slept so long and so well. Then she remembered what her mother called heart-sleep. That sleep a wounded heart needed to help it heal.

She rubbed the ring and medal between her fingers. As she lay quiet, just a few more minutes, she imagined her dad getting up for the day, going down to make the coffee from the beans harvested from the tropics. And her mom coming down to start breakfast.

Everybody up, stock to feed, eggs to gather.

Chores to do, lessons to take, the smell of fresh bread baking. Maybe a trip to the village or the neighboring farms to barter. Free time to read or ride or play.

Where would she be as her family went through the day?

But she, a child of the farm, rose, put on her boots. She added wood to the fire gone to embers and went out to tend to the horses.

She watched the sun rise, as she'd watched it fall.

When she went back in, Mallick had two mugs of strong tea on the counter and fried eggs with bacon in a skillet over the fire, camp-style.

"Good morning," he said. "We'll leave after our breakfast."

"All right." She took the tea—stronger than she liked and more than a little bitter without the honey she preferred.

She wished she'd thought to bring some honey. But she sat with it, and when Mallick put a plate in front of her and sat with her, she ate.

Some of her resentment for him had faded with sleep, but over and above that, she'd grown bored with silence.

"You have no woman or children."

"I don't."

"Is it because you prefer men?"

"No." He continued to eat as he spoke. "My duty, my purpose has been my mate."

"Why would I care, or the gods care, or whatever care if you had a woman, or a man, by your side or in your bed?"

His gaze shifted to hers, held. "What was asked of me, what I vowed, was unswerving loyalty to The One. A mate, a lover, should also have loyalty. And those loyalties might come to odds."

She dismissed that reasoning. "My parents are loyal to each other, and still are loyal to their children. All of us."

"That is love, even more than duty or a vow taken. And love is more powerful."

"You've never loved anybody?"

"There was a girl once, with lively eyes and hair like fire.

I can't say if I felt love, but I felt longing. My heart would pound if I caught sight of her, and if she should smile at me? I was the wealthiest boy in the land. I knew if I ever felt the touch of her hand on my cheek, even just that, I would die happy and fulfilled."

Fallon snorted out a laugh. "Nobody dies from love."

"Oh, but they do, from where love may lead them or what it may ask of them. And so I never felt her hand on my cheek. I made my choice."

"Maybe you did love her because you were a boy, and now you're old, but you remember her." She ate the last of her eggs. "How old are you?"

Mallick sat back, looked her directly in the eyes. "I was born on the third day of the third month in the year six hundred and seventy-one."

"Come on." Out of habit, she started to reach for his plate to clear it. "If you don't want to tell me, just—"

He clamped a hand on her arm. "I was born to a witch, sired by a solider whose own mother had elfin blood. I have little memory of him, as he died in battle when I was barely weaned. I was her only son and, like your mother, she wept when I was called. I had ten years when I left her. And ten more while I trained and studied and traveled. Ten more to practice, to live in solitude.

"Then I slept as the years passed and the world changed, and magicks hid or died as those who held them were persecuted or reviled, or ignored. Until the night I awoke to the sound of a single drop of blood striking the first shield, of the shudder of it cracking beneath the sacrifice. And my time began again as yours would come."

She believed him, and belief made her heart hammer. "You're saying you're immortal."

"No. No. I bleed. My life will come to its end as any man's. But I was asked to train and serve and defend The One, she who would take up the sword and shield, she who would bring the light and restore the balance. I said yes. I took a vow. I made this choice. I will never break that vow. I will never betray you."

He rose, cleared the plates himself.

"What's the first shield and how did it crack under a drop of blood? How many are there? Where are they? How did—"

"You'll learn. For now, gather your things and saddle the horses. I'll deal with the dishes."

"Give me one answer," she demanded. "One damn answer."

"Ask the right question."

She hesitated, then asked what she realized weighed heaviest. "What if I'm not good enough? What if I'm just not good enough or smart enough to do all of this?"

"Then I would have failed. I don't intend to fail. Don't dawdle. We have a long ride ahead."

SHE RODE A FULL hour in silence. Not sulking silence, but thinking silence. She knew some faeries could live more than a hundred years. Like old Lilian at home, who claimed to be a hundred and twenty. Elves could have long lives, too, and children of mixed magicks . . . there hadn't been enough time since the Doom to know for sure.

But she'd never heard of anyone who'd lived for more than a thousand years. He'd said he'd slept, she remembered. Like hibernation?

And if it was all a choice, why had he been called all the way back to train somebody born more than fifteen hundred years later?

It was really confusing. Not understanding wasn't ignorance, she assured herself. It was just not understanding.

They rode through woods, across fields, over roads. Some of the roads still had cars abandoned on them. She saw hills and houses, even a few people, and what she realized was a village, larger than the one she knew, with buildings and the places where they'd once sold gas for cars and food to travelers.

Though for the most part, Mallick stayed off those roads, away from buildings, she'd spot them in the distance.

And wonder.

She'd studied maps and globes and the atlas. She'd seen DVDs that showed a world, showed lives, that seemed so distant and different and exotic.

But the world, once you were out in it, she realized, was so much bigger than anything imagined.

It just went on and on. She couldn't believe it had ever been filled, that cars had streamed along those wide roads she knew had been called highways.

It seemed like make-believe, like the movies on the TV.

"Did you see it?" she asked. "When it was full of people and cars and planes?"

"Yes. And though I had looked in the crystal, though I'd been shown, it was a wonder."

"Is it really a choice, could I have really said no?"

"It's always a choice. I won't betray you, and I won't lie to you."

"Then if you were called so long ago—before there were cars and planes, before the world was so full—how could that happen a zillion years before I was even born?"

"Powers greater than mine, greater than even yours will be, foresaw what might be. It's the nature of people, magickal and not, to wish for peace and march to war. It's the nature of those with darkness in them, more than the light, to plot for war, to covet power. If the dark had failed that night and

73

the shield remained whole, I might have slept another millennium, and The One would not yet be born. But at some point in time, it would happen."

"Did you dream?"

He smiled a little. "I lived lifetimes in dreams. And I learned, even as I slept, of the world and its changes."

"That doesn't seem very restful."

He let out a laugh, rich, full, unexpected. "It wasn't," he told her. "No, it wasn't restful."

Together they crossed a fallow field at a brisk canter, then rode up a steep slope to a blacktopped road.

"How much farther?"

"Another two hours. The rain will come at nightfall, but we'll be there long before."

"Sooner—for the rain," Fallon said.

He gave her a slow, haughty glance. "Is that so?"

"We're riding southeast, and the wind's coming from the east, bringing the rain with it. Unless we change directions, we'll have the rain at least an hour before nightfall if we're traveling this way another two hours at this pace."

She glanced at him with a shrug. "Farmers know the weather. The rest is just math."

He said, "Hmph," and continued to ride.

"Somebody's—"

She broke off when he threw up a hand, as he heard the engines, too. He cursed himself for taking this stretch of the road—to save some time—with little to no cover on either side.

Even as he considered options—the first to lead her in a gallop back over the field—three motorcycles topped the rise of the road, barreled down it.

"If I tell you to go, ride and ride fast, back over the field. I'll find you."

Something in her quivered; something in her steeled. "There are six of them, and one of you."

"There is only one of you in all the world. Do as I say. Do not speak to them, and if I say go, ride."

They rode two to a bike, Fallon noted. Three with sidearms, three with long guns. Four men, two women.

All Raiders, she concluded, with the skull symbols painted on the bikes.

The one in the lead swung his bike across the road so that she and Mallick stopped the horses. He wore a bandanna covered in skulls around his brown hair, a pendant of another around his neck.

He'd groomed his beard into two long tails.

The woman behind him bore the slash of a scar over her left cheek. Like her companions, she wore dark glasses to conceal her eyes.

She tossed a leg over the bike, slung the rifle from her back, and held it in casual threat.

Fallon scanned the others, tried to keep her heartbeat steady as the throaty sound of the engines shut off.

The leader swung off his bike. "Well, what do we have here?"

"My granddaughter and I are traveling south to look for work."

"Is that so? Hear that? They're looking for work."

The one on the second bike tipped down his sunglasses, sent Fallon a wink that made her skin feel sticky.

If she had to fight, she decided to target the woman first, then the winker.

She wouldn't ride away. She would never leave someone so outnumbered.

"What's in the bags?"

"All we have left in the world." The plea in Mallick's voice put Fallon's back up. "And little more than nothing."

"Then you can make do with nothing. Off the horse, Grandpa. You, too, sweetcheeks."

"Please. She's just a child."

The second woman pulled a sidearm. "She gets off the horse or I shoot her off."

"Don't shoot the fresh meat." The one who'd winked got off his bike, rubbed his crotch. "I got some work for her."

They laughed, all, in a way that didn't make Fallon's skin sticky. It turned her mind, her blood, very, very cool.

She dismounted.

"Six of you," she said with disdain. "Two of us."

The leader drew a knife from his belt. "It's about to be one of you."

He lunged at Mallick.

It happened fast, before Fallon could react and she'd thought she was ready.

Mallick's fist flashed out, hard as a hammer strike. He knocked the man back into the woman behind him so they both fell.

With his other hand he hurled a ball of wind that blew the second woman and her sidearm twenty feet back. Even as she landed with a sickening *thud*, Mallick drew a sword.

Two rushed him, and the third left standing ducked aside and charged at Fallon.

She pulled out her knife, and without thinking set it on fire.

"Fucking Uncanny bitch." He snarled at her, drawing his gun. "Bullet beats knife, every time."

"No. It doesn't." She slashed the blade through the air, and the gun in his hand exploded into flames.

When he screamed, dropped it, slapped at the flames over

his hand, she did one of the first defensive moves her father had taught her. She kicked him in the balls.

When he went down, she spun, prepared to help Mallick. He stood with his bloodied sword.

Two lay dead on the ground. The other three were wounded, and the one who'd winked at her was curled up moaning, with a hand she doubted he'd ever have full use of again.

"Collect the weapons," Mallick said briskly.

He bent to take the gun and the knife from the leader. Fallon, feeling a little sick now that it was done, fought to keep her hand steady as she took weapons from the dead.

"That one's gun's melted too much to be of use."

Mallick glanced over where the man moaned, cradled his ruined hand. He said, "Hmph," much as he had about her weather forecast.

She slung one of the rifles over her shoulder by the strap while Mallick took two. After they stowed the other weapons, they remounted.

"You didn't tell me to go."

"Would you have?"

"No."

"Then why would I waste my breath?"

"You may not have taken them all."

"May no longer matters. You have courage. You fought your man well."

"We shouldn't leave them like that. The ones still able might come after us, or hurt someone else."

"We don't kill the unarmed and the wounded."

"No, but . . . " She held out her hand, set the tires on fire.

"Injured, unarmed, and on foot, they won't come after us, and it'll be harder for them to hurt anyone else."

Mallick studied the bikes as they crashed to the ground. "Well done. Good tactics."

"Good sense," she corrected, and began to walk her horse down the road again. Her throat was tight and dry, but she pushed the words out. "They would have killed you. They'd have raped me, then killed me. Or taken me to wherever they were going, raped me again, then killed me. The horses they might've kept if they had use for them, or they'd have slaughtered them for the meat."

"Yes. Unquestionably."

"You killed two of them. Maybe three because the one woman's badly hurt. They'll probably leave her there."

"It troubles you I took their lives?"

"No. Yes," she corrected. "I guess it did, until ... They would have killed us. Not to survive, but because they like it. If we'd just been two people on the road, you'd be dead and I'd be ... We made the right choice."

"They made the wrong choice. Consider this your first lesson."

With a nod, she glanced toward him. "You didn't have a sword before."

"Didn't I?"

"I think I'd have noticed."

He kicked into a canter. "You have to look to see."

HE KEPT THE PACE brisk, following the road before veering off when another settlement came into view. At one point she saw another kind of settlement, one of only houses. Large houses stacked close together, many of them very much the same.

Some had boarded windows, another showed damage from a fire. Deer grazed on the knee-high grass and the wind whistled through the empty streets.

But she saw a shadow at one of the windows. Not all the houses stood empty.

"Why wouldn't people till the ground, grow food?"

"Not all know how," Mallick told her. "Some hide and scavenge. Fear locks them in."

She thought of it as they rode on. More than a hundred houses by her count, and close together for good defense. Wasted, she decided, as the ground that could be planted was wasted.

But as she had on several points along the journey, she marked it in her mind like a signpost on a map.

Once again they moved into a wood with rough, rolling ground where rocks shoved through. She heard the bubble of a stream before she saw it and, with Mallick, followed its meandering flow.

It widened, and water fell frothy and quick over ledges of rock. The rocks climbed higher, the water fell faster so its rushing sound filled the woods.

She spotted a few faeries fluttering in the pale rainbows formed by the strike of the sun on the splashing water.

Beyond the waterfall where its rush softened to a quiet music, Mallick stopped in a wide clearing.

Moss grew heavy on downed trees, lichen on an outcropping of rock. On the edges, trees bowed in an arching canopy.

When Mallick dismounted, Fallon assumed he wanted to rest the horses, so did the same.

"We should be nearly there. We could water them in the stream, walk them awhile, and get where we're going."

"We have."

"Here?" While she had no objection to living in the woods, she didn't relish living without shelter for the next couple years. "We're going to make a camp?"

Saying nothing, Mallick handed her his horse's reins, stepped forward.

He lifted his hands, shoulder high, palms out. For a moment there was nothing but the quiet echo of the waterfall, the shiver of the wind through the trees. The sun angled down, its light slipping through the canopy spilling into the clearing, and shadows shifted with the breath of the wind.

Then she heard the hum of power, felt the first pulse of it on the air, felt it raise the hair on her arms, at the back of her neck. The horses felt it as well and shifted restlessly so she shortened her grip on the reins.

Mallick's eyes deepened so his face seemed to pale as the wind rose up, blowing through his hair, and hers.

Light and shadows changed, shapes formed like a sketch blurred behind rippled glass.

Then his voice rang out, his arms snapped wide.

"Open now what I closed. Reveal here what I cloaked. For this is the place of my making. And The One is come."

The blurred sketch sharpened, took on form and color and shape.

Now in the clearing stood a cottage with a thatched roof and walls the color of sand. Smaller than the farmhouse, larger than the cabin, it had windows facing west and a thick wooden door. Beside it a small stable with a pitched roof held double doors, and close by a small greenhouse shimmered in the stream of sun.

Like the cottage doors, protective symbols had been carved around the frame of the stables, the glass door of the greenhouse.

A statue of the goddess, like the one at the cabin, stood beside the cottage door in a pool of polished stones.

She'd seen her mother's magicks, had practiced her own.

But she'd never witnessed anything approaching the power needed to conceal and conjure on such a scope.

"See to the horses," he told her. "They've had a long journey."

"You're pale."

"It's more difficult to open than to close. See to the horses," he repeated, "then come inside."

He took his pack, walked into the cottage, and shut the door.

Chapter Five

SHE TENDED THE HORSES, AN EASY ENOUGH TASK. THOUGH the stable held only two stalls, they had fresh straw already laid and tools for grooming organized. Both mounts seemed content to settle in with some hay in the basket and the water she fetched from the stream.

She left them to it, carried her duffel, the weapons she'd taken, and what was left of the food her mother had packed to the cottage.

There she paused, remembering, and took her canteen, dribbled water for the goddess on the stones before she opened the cottage door.

It seemed larger inside, and the oddness of it gave her a strange, disorienting sensation. The ceiling rose higher than it should have, the walls spread wider.

A fire burned in the hearth with two sturdy chairs facing it. Rather than a sofa, the room held a wide bench covered in dark brown leather. Candles stood in iron holders on a table. A woven rug spread over the rough planks of the floor.

What served as the kitchen ranged across the back. It held a second, smaller hearth, a worktable, a sink with a window over it. Dried herbs hung in clumps. Jars of roots, berries, mushrooms, and seeds stood together on a wide plank.

She hoped he planned to conjure a stove and a refrigerator. And the power to run them.

But for now he sat by the fire with a glass of what she assumed was wine.

"You have the south-facing room. Leave the weapons on the table. We'll have some food when you've put away your belongings."

"There's no stove, no oven."

"There's a kitchen fire."

"No refrigerator."

"There is the box charmed to keep food cool."

She had a sudden and very bad feeling. "Where's the bathroom?"

"You have a water closet for that need, and both a stream and a well with water for washing."

"Are you kidding me?"

"You will, most certainly, find yourself in places without the advantages you've known until now. You'll learn."

"This already sucks."

She dumped the weapons and, more shocked than angry—no *bathroom*? stomped off to what would be her bedroom.

If she stayed.

At least she didn't have to face lame bunk beds or ugly plaid, she thought with a frowning scan of the tiny bedroom. The bed was a mattress on slats with four short posts, but the blanket on it felt thick and warm.

In lieu of a dresser she had a chest, but she liked the shape of it, liked the painting of three women—goddesses maybe—over it. She had an oil lamp and a rug and a small, square mirror that showed her tired and dissatisfied face.

Still, the window—no curtain—looked out to the woods. She spotted the stone well, which would have saved her the trips to the stream if somebody had bothered to mention it.

She noted a chicken coop, so fresh eggs, and, to her surprise, saw a cow.

So he could do all that, but he couldn't add a damn bathroom?

She didn't bother to unpack, but went back out to complain.

"I want a bathroom. This isn't the seventh century."

"Then you'll have to learn enough to make one. For now, we have what you need to make a stew for dinner, in the cold box and the cupboard."

One shock followed the next. "You want me to cook?"

"I provided your breakfast," he reminded her as he sliced a loaf of bread. "And we have bread and cheese for midday. Your mother taught you to cook. She is an exceptional cook."

"And what do you do when I cook?"

"Eat. We have a cow for milk, chickens for eggs—and meat when needed—a forest for game, and plantings in a greenhouse. You'll eat well enough."

Because she was hungry, she took the bread and cheese. "We need to make a hive. We need to keep bees for honey unless you have a source for sugar. Where do you get the flour and salt and yeast or starter for bread?"

"I barter for it. We'll tend the stock and the plantings together. I have no knowledge of hives, so that will be your task, then you'll teach me how to tend it."

She ate as he did, standing up while they measured each other. "The clearing's too small to hold the house, the stable, the outbuildings. And the house is too small to hold all the rooms in it. You'll teach me how to create that kind of illusion."

"I'm here to teach you."

"If I learn, I want a bathroom. A toilet, a shower, a sink—with hot and cold running water."

He raised his eyebrows. "That seems a great reward for learning."

"What will it take?"

He considered. "I will give you three quests. When you complete all three, you'll have what you want."

"What quests?"

"There is a tree in the wood that bears a single golden apple. A white bird guards it jealously. You'll bring me the apple without harming the bird, bruising the fruit, or climbing the tree."

It sounded amazing—an adventure. But ... "What's the next?"

"Complete the first task, and I'll tell you the second." He wrapped the cheese in a cloth, replaced it in the cold box.

She could find a golden apple, and she could outwit a dumb bird. "What's upstairs where there shouldn't be an upstairs?"

"A workshop and your classroom." He wrapped the bread. "I'll show you, then the cow needs milking, the eggs must be gathered, and you'll want to start the stew."

She wanted to start the hunt for the apple, but decided she could at least look upstairs.

She followed him up a ladder of steps, then struggled not to look amazed. She didn't want to give him the satisfaction.

Carefully labeled bottles filled shelves along one long wall. Potions, she mused while she—as casually as possible—strolled along to study. Ingredients for spells, some of them glowing with magickal light. Books filled the facing wall, and some looked impossibly old. The west wall held tools: cauldrons, athames, bells, bowls, candles, crystals, wands, staffs.

She wanted to touch everything, so she deliberately slipped her hands into her pockets.

A long table and two chairs stood in the room's center. Another hearth, cold now, on the east wall had two closed cupboards flanking it. Over it a mantel held more candles and a sword with a carved hilt.

The only window cut through the roof and let the afternoon sun stream in.

"Here you'll train and learn and practice. And become."

She gestured at the sword over the hearth. "That's not the sword you used before."

"It's not mine to use."

"Mine? Is it the one you told my mother about? The sword and the shield I'm supposed to get?"

"No, but when you're worthy, it will serve you."

"I don't know how to use a sword."

"You'll learn."

She liked the idea of that, and the idea of this room with all its wonders. She liked the idea of finding a golden apple. But she wasn't going to unpack, not yet. She'd give it a week. One week—that was fair. She wanted to find the golden apple and drop it into Mallick's hand. She wanted to learn how to use the sword, and practice magicks she didn't know in the room with the window in the roof.

One week, she thought. Then she'd decide.

SINCE MALLICK FILLED THE rest of the day and well into the evening, Fallon didn't have time to think about decisions. He sent her off to the greenhouse to gather what she needed to add to the venison for stew. She approved of his work there, though she saw room for improvement as she pulled onions, garlic, carrots, some tomatoes, clipped herbs she'd use with the meat and potatoes stored in the cottage.

She thought her mother would be proud of the way she peeled, chopped, mixed. And though Mallick balked at first about using his wine in the stew, Fallon stood firm.

While she set about making egg noodles—something she'd never done on her own—he told her to write down what she needed to build the hive.

"The bees actually build the hive. We build the bee box." She wiped her hands, took the pencil and paper he offered. "It's going to take some scavenging."

"Just write what's needed. I have a way."

Interested, she looked up. "Magickal?"

"Not precisely. When you're done, come upstairs. We'll begin."

HE BEGAN BY TESTING her basic knowledge and skills. Lighting candles, levitating small objects, mixing potions, performing what she thought of as kitchen spells.

Baby stuff to her mind.

Then he started testing her on rituals and deities and symbolism and sabbots.

His opinion of her knowledge was a head shake, a sigh. And a stack of books he pushed into her hands with the order to: Read and learn.

Still, she felt smug when the rain came, as she'd predicted, well before nightfall. And the stew she served over egg noodles was better than okay.

She hoped the next day involved sword practice and the hunt for the golden apple, which would be a lot more fun than cooking and making sleep potions and balms for burns.

She read in her room by the light of an oil lamp until mind and body gave way to fatigue.

At first light she took it upon herself to tend to the horses. When she stepped out she found a package wrapped in brown paper and twine at the front door. Scanning the woods for any movement, she picked it up.

She carried it back inside, set it on the table. Considered. It would be for Mallick, but . . . it didn't have his name on it, did it? And she lived here, too. At least for a week.

Justified, she pulled the twine, pulled back the paper.

A round of cheese, she noted, and sniffed it. A sack of flour, another smaller one of salt, and a corked bottle she assumed was wine.

Mallick came out of his room as she studied them.

"Somebody left this at the door."

"Ah." He looked at the supplies. "We're grateful."

"Who left it? Why?"

"Others live in and around these woods. They're also grateful, and pay tribute. They know The One has come."

"Why wouldn't they knock?"

"They have no need, as yet. Have you fed the horses?"

"No, I was just—"

"See to that. The animals need to be fed before we break our fast."

Rather than swords, Fallon spent most of her morning with books. She liked books, but with the woods so bright and clean from the rain, she'd rather have spent the morning outside learning to fight with a sword.

Still, she liked reading about the gods, the heroism, the betrayals, the battles, and the triumphs, even the romances.

He criticized her lack of knowledge and understanding of the spirituality of the Craft, its rituals.

She bristled. "We had to put food on the table, help our neighbors. My mother taught us what she could, what she knew."

"And did well with what she knew. Did well with what she came to know. You must know more. You'll take what your mother taught you, what I teach you, and what you come to know that's already in you waiting."

He paced the workshop in his soft boots as he spoke, then stopped, pointed one of his long fingers.

"Here's a lesson, Fallon. Your spirit is yours as mine is mine. What you feel and know are yours and will never be a mirror exact of another's. But respect for the spirit and the light, understanding of the dark, must be. And that's shown in the tradition of ritual, in its words, its symbols, its tributes.

"Your power doesn't come from a void, girl. There is a source for the light, for all we are, for the air we breathe, the earth we stand on. Life is a gift, even to a blade of grass, and must be honored. We have been given more, and must honor the gift and the giver."

"When we tend the earth and what it grows, the animals, each other, aren't we honoring?"

"Yes, but more is expected of some than to live an honorable life. Even a simple act can be a symbol. If I offer you my hand, and you take it, it's more than a greeting. It's a gesture of trust, perhaps agreement. My right hand to yours. The hands that hold the sword clasped together in that gesture of trust."

She studied his hand—long like his fingers, and narrow of palm. Then looked up at his face. "Some people are left-handed."

He had to smile, had to nod. "So they are. And there are those who would offer the gesture but not honor its symbol, in whichever hand they hold a sword. So you must learn to judge who to trust. And that is another lesson."

He walked to a shelf, selected a crystal. "What is this?" he asked as he set it in front of her.

"It's ... ah ... bloodstone." She searched her mind. "It's used in healing spells."

"Even before my time soldiers would carry a bloodstone into battle to stop the bleeding from wounds."

"If that's all it took, there wouldn't be so many dead soldiers."

"Your pragmatism is warranted. It takes more than a stone, even a powerful one, and faith to heal. But a ritualized stone, or one used in ritual, one blessed and used in a spell or potion, may heal. That, too, takes faith as well as knowledge and skill."

"My mother's a healer."

"She has that gift."

"She ... yeah, powdered bloodstone mixed with honey and, um, egg whites and rosemary oil."

"Good. The stones are gifts and tools. You must learn how to clean them, charge them, use them. Take from what you see here, make a charm for a restful night, another for a clear mind, and a third for calming a jealous heart. Then you can do as you like until dusk."

He turned toward the steps. "Don't leave the wood," he added. "Don't wander far, and be back at dusk. No later."

She poked around the room a bit. The charms he'd assigned were basic, hardly a challenge, but she wanted to do them perfectly—so to invite a challenge the next time. And she preferred making pouches.

She checked in one of the cupboards beside the fire, found cloth, ribbon, cord, chose what she wanted.

She moved to the other cupboard, and found it locked.

And thought that very interesting.

She lifted a hand—opening a lock wasn't a challenge for her, either—then dropped it again. She'd been raised better. Maybe she could regret that at the moment, faced with a fascinating locked door, but it was simple fact.

Mallick was entitled to his privacy, just as she was.

So, some dried herbs from the jars. Anise, chamomile, lavender, cypress. And bits of crystals. Azurite, aquamarine, citrine, tiger's-eye. Some black pepper, oil of bergamot, of rosemary.

She set out everything in three groups, wrote out simple spells for each on a length of white ribbon, and used a needle to carefully sew the cord through the material to form a pouch. She assembled each one, saying the words on the ribbon three times before adding the ribbon to the pouch, tying it three times.

When she took them downstairs, she didn't see Mallick. Leaving them on the worktable, she got her jacket. Thrilled with the idea of freedom, of the hunt for the apple, she ran outside. She followed the stream for a while, but not the way they'd come, as she hadn't seen an apple tree.

Still, it might not be an apple tree, she considered. That might be part of the trick.

She searched branches, spotted birds—sparrows, jays, cardinals, finches. A hawk's nest, an owl's roost. But no white bird.

She angled away from the stream into thicker trees. She saw tracks and scat of deer, bear, opossum. She saw signs of wild boar and told herself the next time she'd bring her bow. And Grace, she thought. Her horse would get bored after a few days in the stable.

She saw faeries out of the corners of her eyes, but they darted away when she turned. They would be shy yet, she decided, and needed time to get used to her. But she changed direction, following the bright glint of their light into deeper shadows where thick moss covering trees like coats turned those shadows soft, soft green.

In that green light a little pond spread in the deepest of blues with pale green pads floating on it. On one sat a fat frog, apparently dozing, while a dozen dragonflies darted and swooped on long, luminescent wings.

A faerie glade, she realized, as even the air felt happy and sweet.

She sat cross-legged beside the pool, her chin on her fist, and marveled at the glasslike clarity of the water. She could clearly see the bottom, the soft dirt dashed with tiny colored pebbles, the fish, gold and red swimming in the blue.

"It's so pretty here." Leaning forward, she dipped a finger in the pool. "It's warm! Maybe you'll let me swim here."

She'd bring a gift next time, an offering, she decided.

It was so sheltered, not like the stream where she felt exposed when she took off her clothes to wash. Swimming here would be almost as good as—maybe better than—having a shower.

Content for the first time since she'd ridden away from home, she lay back, breathed in.

And saw the apple glinting gold on a high branch overhead.

"Oh my God! I found it."

And the bird, too, she thought as she scrambled to her feet.

Not the dove she'd imagined, but an owl—the biggest she'd ever seen. It sat on the branch beside the apple, and looked down at her with hard eyes of dark gold.

Like Ethan, she could connect with animals, birds, insects, fish. So she tried charm first, smiled.

"Hello! You're really handsome."

The owl stared unblinkingly.

"I'm Fallon. I'm staying in a cottage only a mile or so from here. With Mallick. Maybe you know him."

She heard the titter of faeries, ignored it for now. It wasn't the words, she knew, but the tone, the intent, the images in her own mind.

When the image of herself holding the apple popped into it, the owl spread its great wings, wrapped them around the apple.

She pushed, just a little. She'd been forbidden to harm the owl, and she'd never cause harm to anything so magnificent, but she tried just a little push. Instead of flying off as she'd hoped, he ruffled his feathers and stared down with active dislike.

"All right, okay. God, I want a shower. I want a toilet. You can't imagine how much. Look, I'm The One, and that makes me important. You should want to do me a favor."

He didn't budge, and the next ten minutes of trying to use her mind to trick him into flying away gave her a mild headache.

She needed a plan, she decided. She knew where he was now. She'd work up a plan, come back.

She shrugged as though the owl and the apple meant nothing, strolled away. She'd return, she thought as she moved from green shadows into dappled light. She'd bring a gift for the faeries so she could swim in the pool, and a plan to distract the owl long enough to get the apple.

She said nothing to Mallick about finding the apple, and though for the second night she went to bed with a stack of books, she spent considerable time plotting her strategy.

AND IN THE MORNING, for the second time, she found gifts at the door. Stunned, delighted, she crouched down to examine the wood, the screening, the paint, the nails. The benefactor had even found the slats needed to separate the workers from the queen.

She stood again, stared out into the trees.

"Thanks!" she called. "When we have fresh honey, you can share."

She rushed to muck out the stalls, lay fresh bedding. She reminded Grace they'd take a ride later as she fed and watered both horses.

IN BUILDING THE BEE box, Fallon was the teacher, and she liked it. It balanced out the morning of lessons, instructions, practice—none of which involved swords—and Mallick's less-than-enthusiastic response to her class work.

But for the hive project she took charge because he knew, in her opinion, zippity zip about hives, bees, and honey production.

"We're doing it from the bottom up," she told him once she had the supplies and tools organized to her standards. "So that's the hive stand to keep the hive off the ground. We're going to do an angled landing for the bees."

She had already measured and cut, so she showed Mallick how to lay a bead of wood glue. And found the scent of it reminded her of her dad.

"We have three hives at home. The first one, my grand-mother gave my grandfather the kit and the bees for his birthday the spring before the Doom. The other two I helped Dad build, then the one we built for the ladies at Sisters Farm. They're not really sisters," she said as she worked. "They're witches, really nice, and friends of my mom's especially.

"Now we do the bottom board," she explained. "We're going to use the screen for ventilation, and we need to add the entrance. The bees come and go through the bottom board. So we're making a reducer. It keeps out mice and wasps. Pest and robbers."

She taught well, Mallick thought, working steadily, but explaining each step, guiding him through. She tasked him with constructing a board of slats, for more ventilation, to separate the brood chamber.

"I'm making two medium honey supers. Two's enough just for us, enough to feed the hive, have some for bartering. We're building a queen excluder."

" 'Excluder'?" Mallick frowned. "I thought the queen was vital to the hive."

"She is, but we don't want her laying eggs in the honey, right?"

"I confess I hadn't given that a thought."

"You would if she did. She's bigger than the workers and drones, so we just make the excluder. She can't get into the honey supers, but the bees can get to the queen. We're going to build eight frames for the deep super—that's where they start building their wax. The excluder goes between the deep super and the honey supers."

"Your father taught you all this?"

"Yeah. Well, he had to learn. He read his father's beekeeping books because he didn't do much with the hive until his dad died, so he didn't know much about how it worked. Then we built more. My dad likes to build things. He's really good at it. He built the rooms onto the house and the picnic tables and the . . . "

She trailed off, kept her head down, her hands busy.

"It's natural to miss him, miss your family."

"If I think about it too much it's too hard."

He'd told her he'd never loved, but he had. He'd loved his

mother. Fifteen hundred years didn't kill the memory of his sorrow at leaving her.

His duty was to teach, not to comfort, he thought. And yet, some comfort, some understanding surely paved a path toward teaching.

"What you do here, the sacrifice you make, the knowledge and skills you earn, you do for them. For the world, but they're in the world. What your mother did to keep you safe, what your birth father did, your life father. And they gave you a life, a foundation. Brothers, family. A reason, Fallon, above mere duty to face what comes. They taught you well and gave you knowledge. Enough that you can teach me how to build a home for bees."

"If . . . If I'd said no, would they die?"

"I can't say. I don't know. But you didn't say no. Yet."

She flicked a glance over at him, went back to her work.

She studied his slatted board, approved it, then had him follow her step-by-step as she built one honey super and he the second.

"Okay, this part's really messy. We've got to coat this plastic with beeswax. It gives the bees a start. We need to melt the wax first. I can take it in, melt it over the fire."

Mallick quirked an eyebrow. "Or you could consider this part of the task practice."

She liked that better.

She'd put the two cakes their benefactor had left them in a small cauldron. And now under Mallick's watchful eye, she held her hands over it, glided them down the sides, up again.

He felt the heat, slow and steady, saw the light shimmering from her palms, her fingertips. Soft, pure white.

Inside the cauldron, the wax began to melt.

"What do you call on?"

"The light," she murmured, her gaze fixed on the melting

wax. "The heat. Not fire—not flame. Warmth and light."

"Where does it rise in you?"

"Everywhere. From the belly and . . . below. From the heart and the head. It's through me."

"How do you control it?"

She frowned at that. "I . . . think. Enough to melt, but not to burn or boil. That's enough."

She looked up, smiled. "Now it gets messy."

It took most of the afternoon to build and construct, to paint the exterior a bright white. While Fallon circled around it, crouched down to examine, Mallick stepped back. And found himself foolishly satisfied to have had a part in building something with his own hands.

"It's good," Fallon decreed. "Sound and sturdy."

"You'll give me lessons on the keeping of the bees once we get them. Do they come to the hive, attracted by the box, the wax?"

"You wouldn't get a healthy colony that way, and you'd never draw the queen. You call them, invite them."

"Show me."

"I scouted a colony yesterday. They'll like it here. You've never called bees?"

"No. It's not my gift. Show me," he repeated.

She closed her eyes a moment, a young girl, long-legged, slender, her raven-wing hair in a braid over one shoulder.

"I am in the air, of the air. I am in the light, of the light. I am on the earth, of the earth. I am by the water, of the water. And all these, magicks join. I am of the magicks that join the creatures that walk, that crawl, that fly, that burrow, that swim. We are all of, in, by, on. The queen nests while others brood, work, hunt, build. Here I offer a home, humbly. Come and see. Come and live. Come and thrive."

She spread her arms. "Come."

He saw nothing, heard nothing but the girl, her arms spread wide, her body statue-still. And her face, he thought, luminous.

A minute passed, then another, then a third. He thought to stop her, to tell her she could try again another time.

Then he heard the swarm.

The air filled with a deep, droning buzz, and Fallon stayed still. The cloud, a swirl, swooped out of the woods. His instinct was to rush to her, to pull her away, inside to safety.

Before he moved, she opened her eyes. And glowed.

A large honeybee—the queen?—hovered over the palm of her right hand. And the swarm covered her outstretched arms, her hair, her shoulders, in a mad buzz.

She laughed as though surrounded by butterflies.

Did she know, could she know, all she had? Mallick wondered. All she might be if he didn't fail her? At that moment, her power was so strong, but still young and painfully innocent.

What would she be, what would she hold when that power matured, and that innocence was lost?

She moved then, tipping her fingertips down in a gesture toward the hive. "Welcome," she said. And as one, the swarm entered the hive.

"How do they—" He broke off to steady his voice. "How do they know where they should go inside the hive?"

Her answer came with a puzzled smile. "Well, I told them."

"Ah. All right then, well done. I'll put the tools and so forth away. You're free until dusk."

"I want to take Grace for a ride."

He nodded. "Don't go too far, and be no later than dusk."

She ran off, young, innocent. Mallick listened to the hum of the bees, and felt very old.

BECOMING

Learning is not child's play;
we cannot learn without pain.

—ARISTOTLE

Chapter Six

EVERY DAY FOR THREE DAYS, FALLON VISITED WHAT SHE thought of as faerie-land. She tried magicks on the owl with no success. She tried bribery, intimidation, and what her mother called *reverse psychology*.

I don't want your stupid apple anyway.

He simply sat, guarding the apple that hung tantalizingly from that high branch.

She swam in the pool so at least she felt clean. The little faeries grew used to her and came out to dance or skim along the water when she bathed.

But she couldn't convince any of them to help her get the apple.

She sat on the grass at the end of her first week, drying her hair, studying the stubborn, hard-eyed owl.

She couldn't climb the tree, but what if she went up *without* climbing it? She'd been practicing—away from Mallick's watchful eye—and though her form proved shaky, she'd managed to levitate about two feet off the ground.

The apple, to her gauge, would require a solid ten-foot lift. And then she had to consider that big, sharp beak, those keen talons. So she'd have to practice until she could go high, and go fast.

She wanted to outwit the owl as much on principle now as for the bathroom.

"One week down, a hundred and three weeks to go," she said out loud as she braided her hair.

She still hadn't unpacked, told herself she could leave in the morning, be home in less than two-days' ride.

She didn't mind the lessons and lectures and practice as much as she'd thought she would. Some of it was interesting, even if it had started to cut into her free time since Mallick had added physical training.

Still no sword.

And while she didn't see how being able to balance herself on one hand or juggling balls of light would help her save the whole damn world, she liked learning. She didn't mind the studying or learning about the people Mallick claimed were her ancestors. She liked the spell casting.

But everything took so long, had to be done over and over again. She couldn't imagine spending another one hundred and three weeks doing the same things over and over. Or having nobody but Mallick to talk to.

Maybe she'd try balancing on one hand over the water. Now that would be really interesting. If she could work with two elements—water and air—balance on the surface of the water.

Even Mallick would be impressed.

She would practice levitating in her room with the apple as the goal, and practice the balancing here in faerie-land. When she had perfected those skills, she'd use them as a lever to start learning how to use a sword.

She wished she'd thought of the water-balancing earlier because now she'd already taken most of her free time for the day.

"Tomorrow," she murmured.

She didn't sense or hear anything until almost too late. She spun quickly toward the *sense* in time to see the boy slip half out of a tree, an arrow already notched in his bow.

Even as she threw up a hand in defense, she saw that he aimed the arrow not at her, but at the owl.

She didn't think, only felt. Outrage, fear for another. And the feeling shot her ten feet in the air, slicing out her hand to deflect the arrow. The keen point grazed her palm before the arrow winged away and thudded into another tree. The shock of pain, the shock of rising, broke that feeling. She tumbled back down, landing with enough force to knock her breath away.

"Are you crazy?" The boy, tumbled bronze hair, furious eyes the color of spring leaves, leaped toward her. "I could've killed you."

"Why would you kill the owl? Nobody eats owl."

"You're bleeding. Let me see how bad."

"It's nothing." It hurt like fire, but she knocked his hand away. "You've got no business shooting an arrow in this place, or at the owl."

"I live in this place." He shook back his mop of hair with its single skinny braid falling over his right ear. "Sort of. And I wasn't shooting at the owl."

"Yes, you were!"

"No, I wasn't. Taibhse is a god of the glade. I would never try to hurt him. I was aiming at the apple. You wanted the apple, didn't you?"

"Why would you care?"

"Why not? You'd have the apple now if you hadn't spoiled the shot, and I'd be the one who tricked Taibhse. That's a deep cut. Mallick will have a healing balm. He's a great sorcerer. You're his student."

"And I can take care of myself."

"Whatever." He pulled out a cloth, shoved it at her. "At least wrap it."

Annoyed, she wrapped the cloth around the slice in her palm, pressed her hands hard together, then yanked off the bloodied cloth, tossed it back to him.

The wound had closed, begun to heal.

"Even if you were aiming for the apple, you could have missed, hit the owl."

His chin jerked up. "I don't miss."

"You *did* miss."

"You got in the way." He shrugged it off. "They're saying you're The One, like some great warrior, witch, Savior. You just look like a girl to me."

He wasn't much older than she was, a year, maybe two at the most. Taller, yes, but hardly older. She bristled at having someone her own age so dismissively term her *a girl*.

"If I was just a girl, your arrow wouldn't be stuck in that tree over there."

Pride every bit as much as power had her flinging out a hand, yanking it out, floating it back until it dropped at the base of the owl's tree.

She'd meant to drop it at the boy's feet, but close enough.

"That's pretty good." He walked over to pick it up while the owl stared down at him with cold disdain.

"Look, I was just trying to do you a favor. You've been trying to get that apple for days." Using the cloth, he wiped her blood from the arrow before slipping it back in his quiver.

"It's none of your ... How do you know?" Horror, instant and deeply female, flared through her. "You've been spying on me."

He had the grace to look embarrassed, and it pinked up

the tips of his ears. "I wouldn't call it spying exactly. I just saw you come in here. Nobody outside knows about this place, and nobody who isn't one of us can come into it. So when you could and did, I wanted to see what you were up to."

"You're a, you're a—" She dug for the word. She'd heard it in a movie. "A Peeping Tom."

"I'm Mick. My father's Thomas, but I don't even know any Tom."

"It's an expression."

"What does it mean?"

"A spyer."

"It's not my fault you took your clothes off, and anyway, you're skinny. And I was just trying to do you a favor. You left out sweet cakes."

Her eyes narrowed. "Are you the one who leaves things at the cottage?"

"One of us does. It's tribute, and no payment's expected or needed. It was kind to leave the cakes—and they were good. My father says you repay kindness with kindness, then there's more of it."

"I bet your father wouldn't like knowing you spied on me." She strode to her horse. "Don't do it again. I'll know." She swung onto Grace. "And don't shoot arrows at the owl or the apple. It's not the right way. It's not fair."

She looked down at him, as regally as she could manage after knowing he'd seen her naked. "We appreciate the tribute, so thank you, your father, and whoever else. Now go sneak around somewhere else."

She nudged Grace into a trot.

"Are you coming back tomorrow?" he called out.

She sighed, thought, *Boys*, and declined to answer.

As she approached the edge of the clearing, she heard the

whoosh of wings. She reined in Grace, looked up. Her eyes widened in awe as Taibhse swooped overhead, the stem of the apple in his beak.

Some instinct—Mallick would have termed it a call to her blood—had her lifting an arm. And still it stunned her when the owl glided down, landing on it as if on a branch.

She felt his weight—considerable—but not any bite from his talons. His gold eyes stared into hers, and she felt a connection forged.

Mallick stepped out of the cottage, watched her ride toward him, one hand on the reins, the magnificent owl on her other arm.

Hadn't he dreamed that? Hadn't he seen it? The owl, the ghost god, the hunter, would be hers now. As bound to her, Mallick thought, as he was himself.

"I found the apple. I didn't hurt the owl. He's Taibhse."

"Yes, I know."

"I didn't climb the tree. I don't want to take the apple from him. It's like stealing. But you see I found it, and he can take it back. I want the bathroom, Mallick, but I'm not going to steal to get it."

"You've fulfilled the first quest. The apple is another symbol, Fallon. There are many who would be blinded by the gold and not see the true prize. You've won the loyalty of Taibhse, hunter, guardian, wise spirit. He's yours now as you are his."

"I . . . I can keep him?"

"Girl, he's not to be kept or owned. You belong, one to the other. Lift your arm to release him. He won't go far."

When she lifted her arm, Taibhse soared up, settled on a high branch. When he set the apple down, the stem attached as if the golden fruit had grown there.

"He's beautiful, and brave. What's the second quest?"

"We'll discuss it over dinner. Tend to your horse."

"Don't you want to hear how I got the apple?"

"I do, yes. Over dinner."

THAT NIGHT, SHE UNPACKED and hung Colin's wind chime in her window. On the sill she placed a little jar and set the stem of Ethan's flower in it along with her birth father's book, and the photo of her with her family.

Looking out through the dark, through the dance of faerie lights, she saw the white flash of the great owl on the hunt.

Tomorrow, she thought, she'd hunt, too. After the chores, after the lessons and the practice and the studies, she and Grace would ride the woods on the second quest Mallick had given her. She would find the gold collar, and the wolf who wore it.

WHILE SHE DREAMED, OTHERS hunted. Their fingers probing through the dark scratched at the surface of her dreams. She was the prey, had been since before her birth.

She tossed in sleep, fear urging her to turn away from the images, the voices just beyond reach. Run from them, hide, survive.

What she was pushed to see and hear was blurred and indistinct. To know what to fight.

The circling crows, a gleeful murder heralding death. The flashes of lightning, black for death, red for burning. A circle of stones swimming in fog, and a man wading through it to stand and stare at the scorched and broken earth within the old dance.

The hilt of the sword he carried glinted in a single beam from the moon. Suddenly, his gaze cut away from the stone, and darkly, fiercely green broke through the borders of dreams.

Here the first of seven shields, destroyed by treachery and dark magicks. Here the blood of a son of the gods shed, and here the blood of our blood poisoned. So raged the plague.

Now, Fallon Swift, I wait. We wait. It waits.

He lifted his sword. Lightning struck the lethal point, erupted so he held a blade of white, flashing flame.

Will you take up the sword and the shield of The One? Will you answer the call? Will you come? Will you be?

When he plunged the tip of the sword into the ground, the fog burned. In the stone circle something bubbled and churned.

Choose.

WHILE SHE DREAMED, WHILE others hunted, still others prepared for blood sacrifice.

In what had been, before the Doom, a wealthy suburb in Virginia, a band of Purity Warriors established a base camp. There nearly a hundred men, women, and the children they made, captured, or indoctrinated lived in grand houses and held weekly public executions.

Some, true believers, followed the tenets of Jeremiah White, the cult's founder and self-proclaimed commander. All Uncannys, any who had magickal abilities—or those who sympathized with them—were from hell. Demons and those who trucked with them must be destroyed.

Others joined, bore the symbol of the cult, because they enjoyed the freedom to rape, torture, kill, and a religious fervor baked in blood and bigotry offered the opportunity.

White himself had visited the base. He'd spent two days in one of the grand houses, had given rousing sermons on his twisted god's vengeance, and there presided over the hanging of three prisoners.

An elf, barely twenty, wounded in battle in the outskirts

of D.C. A woman, a healer past seventy, who'd tended the wounds of the elf and others—even those who cursed her for a demon. And a man, simply a man, accused of witchcraft for the crime of trying to protect a child of ten from a beating.

Torture preceded the hanging. White called the screams of the damned trumpet calls to the righteous, and those who followed him cheered in a black wave of hate that rolled like a killing sea.

White traveled with an entourage of bodyguards, strategists, sycophants, and soldiers. And some—if reckless enough or drunk enough—whispered some of that entourage were of the Dark Uncanny.

But White rewarded his faithful with food, slaves, those rousing sermons, and a promise of eternal life when the demon threat was eradicated. So most kept silent.

Sundays, the Sabbath, began with worship. Reverend Charles Booker, formerly a grifter who specialized, with mixed success, in bilking the elderly on home repair and security, led the congregation in prayer and verses from the Old Testament to a god thirsty for blood. Announcements followed the service, given by Kurt Rove, appointed chancellor by White as a reward for his part in the New Hope Massacre. While he ran the base with an iron fist and basked in his position, on Sundays Rove reveled.

Rove might announce changes in laws, often arbitrary. He would read dispatches from White, reports from other bases, from battles, listing numbers killed and captured—this to cheers that celebrated spilled blood.

He would end reading the names of prisoners, and those selected—by committee—for that Sunday's execution.

Attendance to worship, announcements, and Sunday executions was mandatory. Only those assigned guard details were granted dispensation. Illness only served as an excuse for absence if the base doctor, who'd had his medical license revoked before the world ended, issued a waiver.

Those who failed to attend risked, if reported, twenty-four hours in the stocks erected outside the three-car detached garage that served as the prison.

Since Rove's appointment, executions took place at precisely midnight. Not a minute before, not a minute after. "Escorts" selected by lottery led the prisoners from the garage to the public green and the scaffold. Each prisoner bore the brand of a pentagram on their forehead—a Rove flourish White had decreed into Purity Warrior policy. Their hair, roughly shorn, often showed bloody scalps. They were allowed no shoes, only a rough garment of burlap fashioned by slaves.

If the prisoner had wings, they were sliced off. Witches remained as they were since capture, gagged and blindfolded, lest they try to cast their evil eye or speak an incantation.

On this Sunday night, when images of shadows and shapes pushed into Fallon's dreams, as crows circled over the scaffold and those already gathered, two of the six prisoners being held took the forced march.

The witch, raped, beaten, all of her fingers broken, struggled not to limp, not to trip. If she fell, they'd kick her, and they'd already broken her spirit with pain. She was ready to die.

Beside her, fighting to be brave, the shapeshifter, barely twelve, kept his head up. He'd run to draw the hunt away from his little pack. He'd saved his brother and the rest, so he kept reminding himself he wouldn't die a coward.

He could ignore the jeers and taunts of the escort, of the people who ran along the street. He had to ignore the sad, hopeless eyes of the slaves or he might give in to the screaming inside his head.